SCREAMING DIVAS

SUZANNE KAMATA

MeritPress
F+W Media, Inc.

Published by
Merit Press
an imprint of F+W Media, Inc.
10151 Carver Road, Suite 200
Blue Ash, OH 45242. U.S.A.
www.meritpressbooks.com

ISBN 10: 1-4405-7279-8
ISBN 13: 978-1-4405-7279-1
eISBN 10: 1-4405-7280-1
eISBN 13: 978-1-4405-7280-7

Printed in the United States of America.

10 9 8 7 6 5 4 3 2 1

Library of Congress Cataloging-in-Publication Data

Kamata, Suzanne
Screaming Divas / Suzanne Kamata.
pages cm
Summary: A teenage girl–band in 1980s South Carolina becomes a local sensation, but just as its members are about to achieve their rock girl dreams, tragedy strikes.
ISBN 978-1-4405-7279-1 (hc) -- ISBN 1-4405-7279-8 (hc) -- ISBN 978-1-4405-7280-7 (ebook) -- ISBN 1-4405-7280-1 (ebook)
1. Rock groups--Fiction. 2. Bands (Music)--Fiction. I. Title.
PZ7.K12668Sc 2014
[Fic]--dc23
2013045567

Cover design by Frank Rivera.
Cover images © 123RF/Vertes Edmond Minai/gl0ck33.

ACKNOWLEDGMENTS

This book probably would have stayed in a drawer forever if not for the enduring enthusiasm of Helene Dunbar. So, thank you. I'd also like to thank Tracey Waters, Margaret Stawowy, Eric Madeen, Andy Couturier, Leza Lowitz, and Caron Knauer for reading and commenting on earlier drafts. I'm eternally grateful to Pat Conroy and Jonathan Haupt, for their brilliant suggestions; Michelle Sewell of GirlChild Press, for publishing a portion of this book in *Woman's Work: Short Stories*; and the editors of *Hunger Mountain* for publishing another part. I've been deeply honored to work with the fabulous Jacquelyn Mitchard, dream editor and writer extraordinaire, and her wonderful intern, Mary Chamard. Finally, I am so happy to have the support of my fellow SCBWI Japan members, and the UncommonYA writers. I couldn't do this without y'all.

For Helene.

1

Columbia, South Carolina, 1983

Trudy Baxter sank into the back seat of the squad car, her shackled wrists resting lightly on her lap. Outside the windows, fields of tobacco and cotton whizzed by. Mobile homes and loblolly pines wavered in the heat. It was probably a hundred degrees. Better here in this air-conditioned automobile than out there, she thought. Well, almost. She shifted and craned her neck to peer into the rearview mirror. Her lipstick was still bright, hadn't melted. She'd nicked a quality brand. That was weeks ago.

Today they were hauling her away, at her own mother's request, for a pair of sunglasses. She'd been bold—too bold—taking the mirrored lenses into the dressing room along with a pair of jeans. She'd scraped off the price tag with a painted fingernail and perched the glasses on her head like a tiara. When she'd emerged from the curtained cubicle, she'd found a clerk hovering just outside. "Too big." She handed over the jeans without even looking at the middle-aged woman in the faded employee smock, and strutted out the door.

"We'd been watching her for some time," the store manager told the cops later. They were sitting in a little room at the back of the store—Trudy, the policeman, the manager. Trudy's mother, Sarah, sat there chain-smoking. She didn't say a word, but Trudy knew that she was trying to distance herself from the whole scene. Fight the negativity. Focus on the positive. Sarah, the rich Charleston deb-turned-hippie. She was probably imagining peace signs or colors—green, maybe—or sheep.

The shades were ugly. She didn't really want them. She probably would have given them away or ditched them in the parking lot. It was the thrill that she was after, the sweet adrenaline rush.

They'd all had their say. Officer Fred looked from the store manager to Trudy's mother and back again. "So what do y'all want to do?"

Trudy could tell he was hoping for an easy solution. An apology and a few weeks of sweeping up the shop floors, for instance. Maybe he was overdue for a doughnut break, maybe he was sympathetic to her situation. But she knew by the way that the manager avoided her eyes that the woman didn't like her. And she knew all about her mother.

Sarah fixed a cool gaze on her daughter and blew out a long stream of smoke. "Officer, I'm afraid I don't know how to deal with her anymore. I think she needs to be taught a lesson. Why don't you go on ahead and arrest her."

Officer Fred looked to the lady in the smock, registered her timid nod, and sighed. "All right, then. Trudy Baxter, you're under arrest for petty larceny. You have the right to remain silent . . . ."

Riding in the squad car, Trudy looked out and saw a little blue bungalow, like the one she'd lived in when she was small. She thought back to that day when she'd found the For Sale sign stabbed in the front yard. When she'd figured the words out, she'd detonated. Without thinking, she hurled her body against the sign, which hardly budged, a sturdy match for her then-forty-pound body—though it tilted a bit to the left. She stood in the waist-high grass, her chest heaving from the effort, then she launched another attack. That time, she curled her hands into claws and began scraping at the "sold" sticker pasted over the sign.

A door slammed. The scent of cigarette smoke. High heels clattering over the sidewalk. Then Sarah, her mother, was beside her, grabbing her hands, stilling her, looking at the blood.

"Trudy, what has gotten into you?"

"I don't want to move! I want to stay here! Don't make me leave!" She couldn't stop shrieking. She was a thing possessed.

Her mother winced, checked to see if the neighbors were spying at their windows.

"You'll like New Zealand. I promise. There will be lots of fuzzy wuzzy sheep for you to take care of. I'll get you a staff like Little Bo Peep—"

"I don't want to! I don't want to go!"

Every time they moved, the promises were the same: It'll be fun, like summer camp, like Disneyland, like the Island of the Blue Lagoon in that dolphin book that Trudy liked. And always, she was disappointed. When they'd lived in that teepee, the adults had wandered around in a daze, smelling of the pungent cigarettes they puffed. They forgot to cook. Trudy had gone to bed hungry. She'd worn the same clothes for a week. She hadn't had any toys.

Trudy was sick of her mother's adventures. She didn't want any more surprises, any more promises of happily-ever-after. The kids at school teased Trudy about her dirty hair and her hand-me-down clothes and her hippie mother, but she was used to it. She could handle it. She didn't want to live with Baa Baa Black Sheep on the other side of the world. She wanted her pink room and the doll that Grandma Baxter had sent and the dandelions that sprouted in the yard.

"I'm not going. I want to live with Daddy."

Her mother sighed. "Trudy, your daddy did something bad to you. He made you drink bad medicine. You can't live with him."

A month later, Trudy, her little brother Joey, her mother, and her mother's new husband Clifford, got into the Peace Van (thus named because of the mural of Martin Luther King, Nelson Mandela, and Gandhi painted on its side) and left the little white-washed house, with its square yard and red swing set, forever, Trudy shrieking all the while.

She'd shut up when the airplanes came into view. There they were, landing and rising into the sky, a whole flock of them. Trudy had never seen so many airplanes in one place in her life. They had always traveled by the Peace Van, or on foot until someone gave them a ride in the bed of a pickup, or scrunched together in a backseat.

"Kiwis, here we come!" Sarah had one arm hanging out the window. She was waving to every driver they passed.

Trudy knew this mood. Always, it was the same. Sarah, full of hopes for the future, for their new life in the teepees or the nudist camp or the little house in suburbia, sang and danced and bought extravagant presents for her daughter. This time it was a suitcase just for Trudy, filled with frilly dresses and patent leather shoes and a straw hat with plastic daisies on its crown.

Clifford parked the van in short-term parking. He'd already arranged for someone to come and get it. It was sold. They'd probably never ride in it again. Trudy didn't care. She hated that van. The kids at school made fun of it, and it smelled like incense and marijuana and adult sweat.

They walked, each carrying a suitcase—Trudy dragging hers over the asphalt—to the airport. "Departures." (Trudy could read the sign; she was a whiz at reading.) They found the desk for Kiwi Airlines and lined up behind the other people—red-haired, ruddy-faced, thin and fat. Psychedelic dresses, scuffed cowboy boots, frayed jeans, a suit or two. There were all kinds of people waiting to get on that plane.

When it was their turn, Clifford lifted their suitcases onto the luggage conveyor and handed over three blue passports. Trudy still held her suitcase. Clifford must've forgotten it. "Cliff," she said. "Cliff. Cliff!"

He looked back at her then, away from the lady at the counter, then at Sarah, then at Trudy again. Little hills popped out on his forehead.

"You forgot my suitcase," Trudy said, quietly now.

"No, I didn't." Trudy wasn't sure, but it looked like he sneered. He looked away from her to her mother, and something passed between them. They were sharing some secret. Panic fluttered in Trudy's stomach. Why were they making her carry the heavy suitcase? Was it some kind of punishment? And then the thought was pushed aside as they broke away from the line, made their way up the escalator and to the security check.

They walked and walked down a long corridor, and finally Clifford lifted the suitcase out of Trudy's hands. Her mother picked her up, even though she was too big to be carried, and didn't set her down until they reached the waiting area. And who should they find there but Doctor Claire? What was she doing there?

Trudy liked Doctor Claire. She liked her fresh, clean scent and the white coat that she sometimes wore. Trudy liked the little pearl earrings that dotted her earlobes and the smooth, pale skin of her face. Doctor Claire was nice. Sometimes they played together with blocks. Sometimes Trudy colored pictures while Doctor Claire wrote on her yellow paper. And sometimes they talked about Trudy's bad dreams or her father or the mean kids at school.

Trudy ran up to greet her. "We're going to New Zealand," she said. "Are you going, too?"

Doctor Claire looked over her head to where Sarah and Clifford were standing. Her lips pressed together tightly and her eyes narrowed. But when she turned her attention back to Trudy, there was a sweet, sad smile on her face. "No," she said. "We're not going to New Zealand."

Trudy thought that was strange—"we" when it was just Doctor Claire standing alone. She wanted to ask about this, but then her mother came over and hugged her tightly. "Your wish came true, baby. You don't have to go."

None of it made sense. Clifford bent down to kiss her, but she shoved him away. Joey was now in his mother's arms, waving bye-bye. Trudy looked at her suitcase, settled on the floor next to Doctor Claire. She took in the huge airplane outside the window. The crowd was flowing toward the doorway. A young woman in a green jumper was checking tickets. Trudy caught her eye for just a moment and the young woman smiled at her. Then Trudy began running. Her mother and Clifford didn't run after her. They didn't want to miss their plane.

Trudy remembered crying for days, but things were different now. She was tough. All these years later, she knew she could be counted among the girls who clouded up the high school bathroom with their Marlboros, the ones who climbed on the backs of motorcycles with their twentysomething boyfriends, the ones who carried knives in their purses and carved their initials into desks. They acted like nothing could hurt them. No rules could tame them.

Trudy had been so many places—even New Zealand for two miserable months—that the Pine Hills Juvenile Correctional Center seemed like just another way station. How bad could it be? Trudy saw the gates up ahead—like Graceland or something—and the long, groomed stretch of lawn beyond. She felt a surge of hope. They could have picnics here. Play Frisbee! This wouldn't be any worse than that boarding school in England she'd been sent to for a year, or Sarah's old boyfriend's house. At that place, she'd slept on the couch. At least here she'd have her own bed.

She'd put things on the wall or on a bulletin board—her posters of Marilyn Monroe and the Supremes, the little black and white snapshot of her and her father. She'd been a baby then. She didn't remember having her picture taken. She didn't remember her father, either.

They were beyond the gates now, approaching the main building. It was one story, sprawling, your basic no-nonsense design. Something that a kid with blocks might think up. Trudy would have added turrets and gingerbread trim. She liked pretty things.

She'd always imagined herself living in a castle. Someday she'd be a famous model or a rock star and she *would* live in a mansion.

"This is it," her driver announced. His voice had a slightly menacing tone as if she were off to the electric chair. The officer climbed out of the car, opened her door and helped her out by tugging at her elbow. Or maybe he wasn't helping her. Maybe he was afraid she'd run away.

He shoved her down the sidewalk, staring straight ahead. Then he opened the door and yanked her through. A little too rough, Trudy thought. But she kind of liked it. *Trudy Baxter, hardened criminal.* Nobody was going to mess with her in this place.

There were rules at the Pine Hills Juvenile Correctional Center. There were many, many rules. The girls wore green dresses that looked like Girl Scout uniforms. They were not allowed makeup or barrettes (possible weapons) or jewelry. They slept in rows of beds like in the Madeline books Trudy had read as a child. The beds had to be made each day with the covers smoothed out so that not one wrinkle could be seen. They had to polish their shoes. It was like the army, Trudy thought. The rest of the time they studied in locked rooms with barred windows, scribbling equations or capitals of countries on the blackboard. Sometimes they watched nature films.

If the girls got out of line, if they used dirty words or showed bad manners at dinner, they were punished. For milder misdemeanors, a five-page essay might be assigned. Worse infractions could get you thrown into the Quiet Room, a padded cell with a camera in the corner, way up high and out of reach, so they could watch every move you made.

One early summer afternoon the girls were supposed to be picking up trash and pine straw and breathing in the fresh air. Being outside was a great privilege, they were always reminded.

"My sister," a girl said, "lives over at the Women's Correctional Center. She gets to go out four, five times a week on work release."

"Oh, yeah? Is that what happens when you graduate from here?" Trudy and another girl, Lydia, were squatting, combing the ground with their hands, pretending to work.

Lydia was kind of fat and the extra flesh gave her a babyish, innocent look. It was hard to picture her doing something bad.

"What did you do?" Trudy asked her.

Lydia shrugged. A blush colored her pasty skin and Trudy thought, here is a girl who needs her makeup. "I was down at Myrtle Beach with my friends and I met this old man who said he'd give me a hundred dollars if I'd, you know, do it with him."

Trudy raised her eyebrows, impressed. "How old was he?"

Lydia shrugged again. "I don't know. Like, sixty. But I guess he had a rep because some cops'd been watching him. They followed us to the hotel."

"So you didn't actually do anything?" Trudy was a virgin and she thought she might like to talk to someone who wasn't. Find out what it was like.

"Oh, yes, we did. It only took about five minutes. The cops came in right at the end."

"Wow."

"You want to smoke?" Lydia reached into the front of her uniform and pulled out two limp, slightly bent cigarettes.

Trudy took one. "Got a light?"

Lydia extracted a matchbook from her shoe and handed it over.

Trudy had just struck the match, torched the tip of her cigarette, and inhaled deeply when one of the guards stalked up to them.

"Just what do you think you're doing out here, missy? Planning on starting a bonfire?"

Only Trudy was sent to the Quiet Room. She guessed that she had looked guiltier because she was the one with the matches and the lit Marlboro. And Lydia, even if she was a teen prostitute, couldn't help but look innocent with her round, clear face. Lydia didn't make any confessions and Trudy didn't make any accusations. What was the use?

In the Quiet Room there was nothing to do. No TV, no books, no video games. Trudy figured that some girls sat on the floor with their knees hugged to their chests and rocked the hours away. Not her. It would take more than an empty room to break Trudy's spirit. After all she'd been through in her sixteen years—the confusion of step-siblings and foster homes, the constant noise and lack of privacy—the Quiet Room was almost a refuge. Even so, she started to get bored after a while. She decided to sing, remembering how songs had made long trips in the Peace Van seem shorter than they really were.

She started with "Stop! In the Name of Love." She knew the words to every song by Diana Ross and the Supremes, that great girl group of the 1960s. Sarah had been a big Motown freak. It was the only thing she'd passed on to her daughter.

Once Trudy's mother had married a black man, Alphonse, from Bermuda. (He'd been husband number three.)

"I wish I could be black like you," she told him.

"Why's that?" He smiled—a string of pearls. He was used to her non sequiturs, her weird musings.

"If I was black, I could be a Supreme."

Alphonse laughed. "Oh, it's not that much fun. Look at what happened to Flo. Turned into an alcoholic and drank herself to death."

In Trudy's mind, Florence Ballard was still alive. As long as her voice continued to flow from the stereo speakers and her picture was still on the album cover, she was there.

In the Quiet Room, Trudy took the part of Diana Ross and launched into song. She sang "Baby Love" and "I Hear a Symphony" and "Come See About Me." Then she sang "Chain Gang," which had really been Sam Cooke's song, but the Supremes had covered it. She sang this one especially loud since it was a prison song, and wasn't this prison?

The next time she got tossed into the Quiet Room was for cursing at one of the teachers. The lesson had been boring, something about checks and balances, and Trudy was glad to get out of there. This time she just curled up on a corner of the dusty floor and took a nap.

The door opened about an hour later.

"Wake up!" The guard stood there.

Trudy couldn't believe the time had passed so quickly. She rubbed the sleep from her eyes and pulled her skirt over her legs. A sour taste was in her mouth. Her stomach rumbled. Suppertime?

"Your father is here to see you," the woman said.

"My father?" It must be some kind of a joke. Trudy hadn't seen Jack, her biological father, since the divorce. According to Sarah, Jack had slipped some acid into her Kool-Aid during an adult party. Trudy had freaked out and Jack was banished from their lives.

None of her stepfathers had ever been to visit her. Her mother's latest husband didn't even like her. That's why she was living in this hole. She was smart enough to figure that out.

She followed the guard out of the tiny cell into the corridor. In the waiting room, she saw him. He was standing, facing away from her, reading a notice posted to the wall. Something about holiday leave and what kind of presents parents were allowed to bring. The man was slim-hipped, dressed down in faded jeans and a black T-shirt. His black hair rippled over his shoulders like some hairdo in an old Italian painting. When he turned, when she saw that face—the kind dark eyes and the fleshy lips, the too-big nose that hooked like a beak—she recognized him. Her heart hammered.

"Dad, where the hell have you been?"

He regarded her warily, as if he wasn't quite sure he had the right girl. Then he lifted his hands, palms out. "Your mother wouldn't let me near you," he said. "She took out a court order. You knew that, didn't you?"

Trudy stood stiffly, her chin angled upwards. It's got to be a lie, she thought. She wanted to believe him, but she'd been betrayed so many times in her life that it was next to impossible to have faith in this man. "All I know is that you abandoned me."

He looked stricken then. His face seemed to sag, and Trudy wondered for a moment if he would cry. Well, good. He deserved to suffer. She wanted a cigarette badly.

"Got a smoke?" she asked.

He shook his head. Stared at the floor. "Trudy, I—I wrote to you. Didn't you get my letters?"

"Nope. Not a one. But I've moved a lot. Maybe they just didn't get to me." She could see how disappointed he was. What had he expected? She'd fly into his arms—"Oh, Daddy!"—and it would be happily-ever-after from hereon out? Afraid not. Yet, he was here and she had a chance to get something from him, something to make up for twelve years of neglect.

"Can you get me out of here?"

He looked at her then. "Yes. Yes, of course. You don't belong here. I don't know what Sarah was thinking. You'll come home with me."

Trudy nodded. "Do you have a wife? Kids?"

"No, there's just Ginny, my girlfriend, but she doesn't live with me. And if you get to know her, I think you'll get along fine."

"You don't know the first thing about me," Trudy wanted to say. But she didn't. She kept her mouth shut. This man was her ticket out of that hellhole. No more Quiet Room. No more bed-making inspections. If she didn't like her dad's place, she'd leave. She was old enough to get by on her own. She thought of Lydia, chubby Lydia who'd made a hundred dollars just by spreading her legs for five minutes.

Her dad went off to fill out some papers, and Trudy was sent to collect her things. The room was empty. Everyone else was off doing arts and crafts. Trudy opened the footlocker she'd kept beneath her bed and grabbed a handful of underwear, stuffed it in her duffel bag. She didn't bother folding the T-shirts, the jeans, the other Saturday-only clothes, just crammed them into the bag and zipped it shut. Then she carefully unpinned the pictures from her allotted twelve inch by twelve inch corkboard—the magazine pictures of Marilyn on her back, bench-pressing a barbell, the Supremes in matching spangly outfits, the black and white picture of her father with short hair, wearing bell-bottomed pants and with Trudy in his arms. She tucked the pictures into the outer pocket of her duffel bag.

When she left, there'd be no trace of her. The bed with its plain blue coverlet would belong to someone else. Another girl would stow her panties in that latched chest. Trudy wished she had a knife so that she could carve her initials somewhere. Then someone would know that she'd been part of this place, if only for a short time.

2

Harumi Yokoyama and her mother were not exotic in New York City. So far since arriving, Harumi had seen the following: a raggedy man yelling at God. A six-foot-tall transvestite with cocoa skin, a curly wig, and a feather boa tossed over his/her quarterback shoulders. A movie star flicking her cigarette out the window of a limo. And there were Asians everywhere: Chinese boys ferrying moo goo gai pan through the city on their bicycles. Wrinkled grannies with babies on their backs, just like in the old country. No one treated Harumi's mother like an imbecile when she mixed up her verbs or made mistakes in grammar. No one scrunched their eyebrows together, trying to make out her accent. In certain neighborhoods, Mrs. Yokoyama spoke in Japanese and was understood.

"*Oishii!*" she said, as they sat in the Sakura Garden eating sushi.

The waitress smiled. She wore a kimono and the bun at the back of her head was studded with decorative sticks. "I'm glad you like it."

"*O-cha o kudasai,*" Mrs. Yokoyama called out the next time she walked by.

The waitress disappeared for a moment, and came back with a pot of tea. She bowed slightly, then with one hand on the lid of the teapot, poured light green liquid into stoneware cups.

"Just like Japan," Mrs. Yokoyama said to her daughter across the table, her face all aglow.

"*Kincho shite imasu ka?*" she asked.

"No, I'm not tense," Harumi lied. She got nervous before every performance, no matter how minor. Whether she was soloing or playing along with the rest of the orchestra, she always worried that she would make a mistake. She was afraid that she would suddenly forget how to read the black notes on the page in front of her, or that her fingers would cramp and freeze.

Today there wouldn't be an auditorium full of people. There'd be five or six, maybe. It would be like playing to her mother's Friday lunch group or to the few relatives that gathered during the New Year's holiday. She'd be alone, onstage, and she could look out into the depths of the theater and pretend that she was playing for herself.

She had practiced for this day for months now. Hashimoto-sensei had helped her choose the piece that she would perform for her audition to the most famous music school in America. She had sat and listened to her star pupil play Schubert's "Rondo in A" over and over again. "A little slower there," she'd say. Or "*Fortissimo!* Louder!" When Harumi had finally gotten it right, Hashimoto-sensei had broken down in tears. "I can't help you anymore," she said. "You've learned all that I can teach you." So now it was time for a higher level of instruction. Professionals would guide Harumi to a career as a concert violinist. She would cut records and appear on PBS.

Harumi dreamed in music. She sawed at her violin all night long, her strings sometimes snapping and flying off the instrument. Her fingers formed chords as she slept. "Rondo in A" had been the soundtrack for her life over the past few months.

"This will give you strength," Mrs. Yokoyama said, scooping a mouthful of rice with her chopsticks.

But Harumi's stomach was in revolt. She could manage only a few bites of sea bream on vinegared rice and a sip or two of miso soup.

"Tonight we will have *shabu-shabu*," Mrs. Yokoyama said, already thinking about celebrating. "I saw a place for it in my guidebook."

Is this what life would be like in New York? Being led from Japanese restaurant to Japanese restaurant like a dog on a leash? If she were accepted into the music program, she would have to live in the city with a guardian. Mrs. Yokoyama had already declared that she would be willing to look after her daughter, leaving her architect husband and son to fend for themselves in their home down south. They would see each other on weekends and holidays. They would spend all summer together, maybe at Coney Island. It would be lonely, especially at first, but the sacrifice was worth it. Harumi had been born with a glorious gift and her parents agreed that it was their responsibility to do everything in their power to help their oldest child develop her talents.

Harumi knew about sacrifices. She'd given up jazz dance and the photography club and shopping and TV. She'd given up her friends, too, all so that she could become the best young violinist in the state. She was a freak, not even remotely aware of the latest movie or high school gossip. She didn't even know what kind of music was popular. Sometimes this made her feel incredibly lonely. At school, she felt a pang when she passed Esther Shealy in the hallway. They'd once been like sisters. Esther had even beaten up a kid in defense of her honor. But her parents had quashed the friendship. They pretended to forget to pass on Esther's phone messages until she stopped calling altogether. And when Esther dropped by on her bicycle, they told her that Harumi was practicing her violin. As for boys—forget it. Harumi was forbidden to date until she was eighteen.

"Look at handsome guy," her mother stage-whispered in the sushi restaurant. This was her attempt to make up for all the girl talk Harumi missed among her peers.

Harumi's eyes followed the direction of her mother's nod. A young Japanese man in a well-cut suit was settling in at a booth near the door. He had smooth hairless skin and slicked back hair. Even from across the room, Harumi could see that his fingernails were manicured. He looked the picture of success. And he was Japanese. Husband material.

Harumi didn't think her mother had ever had a fling. She might have had a few harmless crushes in her girlhood, but as soon as she'd been old enough for dating, her mind had been on marriage. She'd married fresh out of an all-girls college, at the age of twenty-two.

Harumi had heard the story of their courtship plenty of times. A friend of the family had brought over a young man visiting from America, where he was studying to be an architect. Her mother, who had never had a boyfriend before, had been smitten at first sight. Letters were exchanged. On his next visit a wedding was hastily arranged, and she went back with him to a tiny roach-infested apartment in married housing.

Probably the idea of life abroad had seemed exotic at first, but these days her mother's dreams were about going back to Japan. They all knew, however, that architects didn't make as much money there as in the States, nor did they have the same kind of prestige. Plus, after a certain age, it was hard to start over. So they stayed in America.

Sometimes Harumi wondered if her mother wished she had married someone else. She was sure that she'd never slept with anyone other than her husband.

Harumi suddenly felt dizzy. She was nervous and she hadn't eaten, but there was more to it than that. Her life was like a box and Mrs. Yokoyama was hammering down the lid. Everything had already been decided by others who claimed to know what was best for her. No one had ever asked her what she wanted. Maybe she just wanted to take her violin out on the back porch and play for the crickets. Maybe she wanted to sprawl across Esther Shealy's bed watching *General Hospital* and eating marshmallow pies. Maybe she had no interest in living in a tiny walk-up apartment in New York, far from her brother and father.

After a few more mouthfuls, Harumi pushed her plates away and followed her mother out of the restaurant. They went back to the hotel where Harumi changed from jeans and a polo shirt into a blazer and skirt.

"You look very nice," her mother said. "Very serious. Do you want to practice some more before we go?"

Harumi shook her head. "No, I'm ready. Ready as I ever will be." She grabbed her violin case and headed for the door.

There was a line of nervous mothers and their children at the school. Harumi registered at a long table and took her place in the queue. The others—ranging in age from about twelve to eighteen, and in color from pearl to ebony—eyed her suspiciously. Friendly conversation didn't seem likely.

Harumi slumped into a chair. She cradled Sadie II in her arms, as if it were a baby in need of a lullaby. She remembered the day that she had traded in her first violin for the full-sized one she used now. It had been nearly a ceremony. Hashimoto-sensei, the music shop clerk, her mother and father, and even her brother had stood around her as she first fondled the instrument. They'd watched her stroke the strings with her horsehair bow and strained to catch each plaintive note. Everyone knew that Harumi was destined for great things, that she'd be a guest of the Carolina Symphony, and that in the future, they might be asked to recount this day for some journalist.

Harumi had tried several instruments before she found the right one. No one else would have been able to tell the difference, but when Harumi hoisted this one onto her shoulder, it fit just right. When she plucked the strings, they seemed to be communicating with her. This was Sadie II.

At the end of the line, a boy wearing a necktie and horn-rimmed glasses unzipped his cello from its case. He stood perfectly straight while his mother licked her finger and smoothed back a stray lock of hair. The mother looked ordinary. She wore orthopedic shoes and a suit two or three years out of fashion. Harumi wondered if all of that family's fortunes depended upon the boy. Had they poured all of their savings into his future? Were those slender shoulders strong enough to support the weight of their expectations?

Harumi felt sick to her stomach. She'd heard stories about dutiful Japanese daughters, girls who devoted their lives to caring for sick parents. They gave up on careers, on love, on motherhood, to play nurse. And then when the parents died, they had nothing left in their lives. But her parents weren't sick. Her father's salary was enough to feed and clothe them and keep them in a house with a swimming pool. Her father hadn't said a word when his wife made a reservation at the Savoy.

"Go see a show on Broadway, too," he'd said, pressing his credit card into her hand.

Harumi's parents could get by without her. They were greedy, that's all. They wanted a famous daughter to make up for every humiliation they had suffered as a member of a minority in America. With Harumi's success, they would be able to rise above the Confederate flag bumper stickers, the slurs of Jap/Chink/Gook, the fact that Harumi's mother hadn't been invited to join the Junior League or the Garden Club.

She looks so smug, Harumi thought, looking over at her. All of that praise directed at me has gone to her head.

"Harumi Yokoyama!"

Harumi startled at the sound of her name. She hadn't noticed that the three in front of her had already finished their auditions.

Mrs. Yokoyama nudged her out of her seat. "*Ganbatte*," she said. "Do your best."

Harumi took a deep breath and strode toward the stage door. She nodded to the man with the clipboard, and went out onto the bare stage. There were no chairs, no music stands, only a pool of light. Harumi stepped into the beam and took her instrument out of its case.

"We're ready when you are," a voice called from the shadows just beyond the stage. The voice was gentle and patient, seemingly disembodied. If she looked carefully, she might have been able to make out the figures seated there, but she chose to ignore them. She pretended that she was alone in a forest, far away from New York City.

Harumi lifted Sadie II onto her shoulder, the gesture almost second nature by now. She picked up her bow, her fingers forming a fox's head. And then she launched her bow-turned-rocket and began wheedling sweet music from the strings. Her touch was perfect and she felt herself flowing with the notes, her spirit soaring through the treetops. Her body swayed with the melody, as if she were dancing with an invisible lover.

But then a black crow flew into her thoughts. She became aware of the judges sitting in the dark, of her mother praying on a folding chair. She became aware of the dim theater and it suddenly seemed like a jail. If she kept playing, this would be her home.

Harumi's playing became more furious, more beautiful. It was as if the music had a mind of its own. She had to stop. She had to let the bow fall from her fingers and clatter to the hardwood floor. She had to tell those invisible judges that she wouldn't play for them. And so she summoned all of her strength, siphoned it from the music, from the deepest part of her, and raised Sadie II high into the air.

She closed her eyes and cupped her hands over her ears as the violin smashed and splintered on the floor.

3

Cassie Haywood was in her room, listening to Billie Holiday, smoothing foundation over the scythe-shaped scar that ran along the right side of her face. It was the same kind of special heavy-duty makeup that had been used on her mother after the accident. Before they put her in the ground. In another couple of years, she could have cosmetic surgery again. She'd never be able to wear a bikini, but maybe something could be done about her face. Her broken heart was another story; that could never be fixed.

"You're a beautiful girl," her father always told her. "So what if you don't have a crown."

She knew that even though he had married a beauty queen himself, he had never approved of the pageants. He was unimpressed by her titles—Miss Peach Blossom, Little Miss Chitlin Strut—and her once-possible future appearance in Atlantic City. Others squealed over her sausage curls and vocal talent, but her father always said that there was something sick about parading a five-year-old around in sequins and mascara.

"Then why did you let her make me go up on all those stages?" Cassie hadn't minded. She'd loved having her mama fuss with her hair before she went onstage to sing, the heft of the gold cups, the sparkle of the crowns. She hadn't known anything different.

Her father shrugged. He didn't like to talk about his first wife, Cassie's mother.

A motor rumbled outside and Cassie turned to the window. She pulled the curtain back. A red Mustang was idling in the driveway. After a moment, the engine cut off. The door swung open and there he was, Todd Elsworth, star quarterback at Irmo High School. He stepped out onto the driveway and marched to the front door.

Cassie pulled away from the window and fluffed up her hair. She'd dressed casually in a black miniskirt and an oversized red sweatshirt that grazed her thighs. They were just going to a movie—no need to get too dressed up, even if it was a first date.

Billie's voice drowned out the sound of the doorbell. Cassie stayed in her room till she heard Johnette shouting up the stairs for her. *Better get down there before she starts flirting with him.* Cassie turned off the stereo, grabbed her pocketbook, and left the room.

She found them in the living room—Todd sunk into one of the plush arm chairs, a Coke in hand, and Johnette on the edge of the sofa, leaning toward him.

"Okay, I'm ready," Cassie said loudly. "Tell Dad I won't be out late."

Johnette jumped, surprised, then recovered. "You kids have a good time," she said. "No drinking and driving, Todd."

Cassie slit her eyes at Johnette before shooting out the door. Why did she always have to make allusions? And why did she have to fawn all over Cassie's dates? Was she sorry she'd married a much older man?

"That's your mother?" Todd asked once they were in the car.

"My stepmother."

"She doesn't look like anybody's mother." Todd's eyes were a little too bright. "She's . . . she's gorgeous."

They all said that—all the zit-faced boys who climbed the steps to her front door. They were floored by Johnette's teased honey tresses, her firm Nautilus-trained figure, her huge green eyes. She was your basic thirty-two-year-old trophy wife.

Cassie sighed. "She's married, so get over it."

"I didn't mean it like that. C'mon. Don't get mad. You're gorgeous, too. I don't care about your scar. I think you're the prettiest girl at school."

"Gee, thanks."

Cassie remembered the first time her father had brought Johnette home. He'd met her at the health club where he'd started working out, on his doctor's advice. Johnette had probably been impressed by her father's air of wealth and sophistication. And then there was the sob story about the tragic car accident, the dead wife, the motherless waif. Women always fell for that.

Cassie's father Dex, short for Dexter, threw open the door one evening and called out, "Honey, I've got a surprise for you!"

Cassie had rushed down the stairs, expecting a new car or maybe a puppy. Whatever. She'd stood in the living room, curious, while her father started up a drum roll on the doorframe. His eyes were on something in the driveway, out of Cassie's field of vision. Then he did his *Tonight Show* introduction: "Heeeerrrrre's Johnette!"

A giggling blonde stepped into the room. It was summer and she was wearing a skinny-strapped sundress splashed with bright pink flowers.

Cassie couldn't fit everything together at first. Was this some secret love child? A singing telegram? Her father's last girlfriend had been a divorced junior high teacher with kids Cassie's age.

"Um, hi," she said, as Johnette pulled her into a hug. The woman reeked of Chanel No. 5. "Dad?"

"This is my fiancée." He was wearing a goofy grin. Cassie was sure that he was drunk or maybe even stoned, but later, when the three of them sat down to dinner, he proudly assured her that his bride-to-be never drank alcohol.

"I'm strictly vegetarian," she said. "Macrobiotics have changed my life."

"Great."

They'd gotten married in Hawaii, sparing the family the embarrassment of a church wedding. Ever since then, there'd been plenty of tofu and carrot juice in the refrigerator. Stacks of yoga videos flanked the TV. Brightly colored jogging bras and skimpy lingerie spilled out of the laundry basket.

And now, sitting here with Todd drooling over Johnette's image, she suddenly didn't want to be on this date. She didn't want to sit in a dark movie theater for an hour and a half while his hand inched slowly toward her thigh.

"I've got an idea," she said.

"What's that?"

"Why don't we forget about the movie and go to The Cave. You know, that new club downtown? I heard they don't card at the door."

"The Cave?" He frowned. "It's full of freaks. Drug addicts."

Todd roamed the halls in his perfect world, but he didn't know about much besides football and prom and teenage keg parties. She wanted to shock him. "You ever heard of slumming? Sometimes it's really fun."

Cassie had been to The Cave a few times before. The first was with a group of friends after a football game. Rhonda and Lisa had remained stuck to the wall, giggling in the shadows, amazed at their own bravado. Cassie, however, felt right at home. In the dark, no one could see her scar. They were all wounded in some way, she thought, looking at the figures in black around her. She saw the way that their bodies banged and thrashed to the music. They were dancing through their fears. She could do the same.

"How about we go after the movie?" Todd suggested.

Maybe he'd heard things and was scared to go. Needed time to buck up his courage.

"Okay." Cassie resigned herself to being a hostage. "Whatever."

They went into the theater and Todd paid for the tickets. He bought a large popcorn for them to share—oh, how romantic. Cassie carried the Cokes. When they were settled into the burgundy velvet seats and the lights had gone down, Todd pulled something out of his jacket pocket. The silver flask caught light from the screen and flashed briefly. "I've got a surprise," he whispered.

Cassie watched him unscrew the top and caught a whiff of whiskey. Ugh. Anything but that. She turned away and covered her mouth.

"What's wrong?"

Didn't he know about her mother? Didn't he know what whiskey had done to her face?

"Maybe you should take me home," she said, not bothering to lower her voice. She'd thought, when he'd first asked her out, that she might sleep with him. She'd been attracted by his hooded eyes and dimpled chin. Plus, there was that muscle-packed body. But now she knew that she wouldn't.

Cassie didn't know why she bothered with high school boys at all. Todd was just like all the rest, incapable of understanding her. Now he was twisting the cap back onto the flask, tucking it back into his jacket. He reached for her hand. She pretended not to notice.

"Sorry, Cassie. You said you wanted to go to The Cave, so I thought you'd be into it."

Someone behind them made a shushing noise and they settled in to watch the movie.

On a scale of one to ten, the movie was a zero. There were a bunch of men racing around in cars, talking about tits and ass. Todd laughed. Once in a while he looked over at Cassie, hoping to catch her eye, but she kept her eyes on the screen.

They didn't go to The Cave after all. Todd knew about some party out on Lake Murray.

"Fine. Whatever." Maybe she'd meet some cool people. Maybe she could ditch Todd and find her own way home. He was turning out to be a brainless bore.

As he drove through the night, ten miles over the speed limit all the way, he did a recap of his favorite scenes from the movie.

"Wasn't it awesome the way the Mustang flew off that ramp and landed nose first in the cow pasture?"

"Yeah," Cassie said, "and then they just drove off into the sunset. In real life they'd all have been crushed."

Todd shook his head. "You're so morbid."

The party house was out in the middle of nowhere. Todd drove through dense forest along a dirt two-track road till they reached the end of a row of cars parked haphazardly along the driveway. Ferns and saplings had been mowed over to make room for sports cars and primer-stained jalopies. There were a couple of sedans that screamed "Daddy's" and Cassie wondered how the parents would react in the morning to the scratches and dents and puke on the upholstery.

"Whose party is this?" Cassie asked, before jumping out of the car.

"I don't know. A guy on the team heard about it. He told me it'd be rockin'."

"We'll see," Cassie murmured. She followed Todd down the last stretch of dirt road to the house.

The place was lit up like a Christmas tree and music was leaking out into the night. Cassie could hear a guttural voice and the energetic strumming of a bass guitar.

She recognized some of the kids that she saw from school. A couple of cheerleaders, too drunk to walk alone, were staggering toward the row of cars. Cassie imagined one of them sticking a key in the ignition and shuddered.

One of Todd's football buddies was making out with some girl on the hood of a car. Todd slapped him on the butt and he came up for air for a second. "Yo, Todd! Way to go," he said leering at Cassie. Then he turned back to the girl, probably someone he wouldn't even talk to on a regular day at school.

Cassie pushed through the door. The living room was jam-packed with hot bodies. They pogoed and slammed, making the house shake on its foundation. All furniture had been removed. The carpet was wet in spots from spilled beer.

The band was in the corner of the room. A skinhead boy from her physics class was wailing on the drums. His timing was off, but nobody cared. The lead singer stomped around in a small square of space, shouting obscenities and cryptic phrases. His hair was shoe-polish black and slicked down against his skull. He wore a ripped white T-shirt, and his skinny tattooed arms flailed around as he screamed. Once in a while he picked up a guitar and thrashed its strings. Scary guy, Cassie thought. Todd would probably think he was a freak.

Off to the side, a girl with long black hair falling over her face was bent over a bass guitar. She seemed oblivious to everyone else in the room, her attention centered on her fingers and strings. She was the only one of them, Cassie realized, who knew what she was doing. The girl, dressed in a baggy housedress like Cassie's grandmother sometimes wore, didn't look up until the song—or whatever—was finished. When she raised her head, Cassie saw her delicately boned face, her angry Asian eyes. Harumi Yokoyama. No way. Harumi in a punk band?

Cassie didn't know Harumi personally, but she knew about her. Everyone did. She was some kind of child prodigy and she was always winning awards. Like Cassie, she'd spent a lot of her early years performing in front of audiences. Harumi had kept going, though, while Cassie's singing career had been cut short. There had been rumors about Harumi going to Juilliard and on concert tours. In her newspaper photos, she always looked completely proper in crewneck sweaters and plaid skirts, but Cassie had always seen something fierce in her eyes. The fire of ambition, she'd thought. But now, looking at her in that lake house living room, she thought that maybe the look was about something else.

"We're going to take a break," the leader screamed. "Let's refuel!" He grabbed a bottle of beer and poured it over his head, then into his mouth.

Cassie had almost forgotten about Todd, but now she saw him across the room, talking to some girl with big blonde hair. She had her hand on his bicep as she laughed at something that he said. Cassie saw Todd look through the haze of cigarette and marijuana smoke at her. She realized that he was trying to make her jealous. Ha.

She wove her way through the crowd, pushed open the sliding glass doors and slipped into the night. She found herself on the deck and stepped to the railing. The wind was moving through the trees. Down a slight incline, waves lapped at the beach.

There was a couple groping each other in a shadowy corner. They weren't making much noise. It was almost like being alone, standing there looking into the dark. Then the sliding glass door opened again, and music blared out to her.

Cassie turned to see Harumi stretching her arms toward the moon.

"Hey," Cassie said. "You were great in there." It was probably a stupid thing to say to a concert musician. Harumi was famous for being good at music. Still, she wanted to say something and she didn't know what else to say.

"Thanks." Harumi moved to the railing, so close that Cassie could feel her body heat. "Sometimes those guys can be morons, though." She nodded toward the living room where her bandmates were chugging beer.

"Yeah, I know what you mean," Cassie said. "High school boys."

"I saw you come in with Todd. Are you dating him?"

Cassie glanced at Harumi's face. There was no derision there, only curiosity. It was amazing that Harumi had even noticed, amazing that she knew who Cassie and Todd were. She'd always thought that Harumi was beyond high school cliques and gossip, off in a world of her own.

"I don't think I'll ever go out with him again."

Harumi laughed.

They both turned and looked through the window. Todd was kissing the girl with the big blonde hair.

"Do you want me to give you a ride home?" Harumi asked.

"What about the band? Aren't you going to play another set?"

Harumi shrugged. "They'll probably be too drunk for that. Or at least too drunk to care whether I'm here or not."

Cassie waited on the deck while Harumi went inside to get her bass. No one seemed to be paying attention to her. No one realized that she was leaving. No one, that is, except for Todd. Cassie saw Harumi tap him on the back. He turned around, the blonde's hands on his chest, and leaned his ear toward Harumi.

Almost as soon as Harumi veered away from him, he shook off the other girl's hands and forced his way through the crowd.

Oh, great. He's going to try to be manly and claim his woman now. Cassie ducked under the railing and jumped to the ground, then snuck around to the front of the house where the cars were parked. She hunkered down behind a Jeep until she saw Harumi appear.

"Let's get out of here," Harumi said.

4

"Dear Cassandra," Esther Shealy wrote. "Have I ever told you how beautiful I think you are?

"The Japanese believe that something that is perfect cannot be beautiful. Sometimes a potter will deliberately make a vase lopsided because it's more interesting that way. Or the guy (or woman) will put a scratch in it or chip it after it's finished. My Japanese-American friend told me all this and I know it's true.

"I think that your heart is probably beautiful, too, in a damaged kind of way. I hope you don't mind me saying all this. I only write these things because I care about you and think about you all the time.

"As always, I love you."

Esther put down her pen and folded the paper. She closed her eyes and tried to block out the sounds of her brother Mark's stereo coming from the other side of the wall. She was alone in her room, the desk lamp her only source of light. Her clothes were piled on the floor, twisted and wrinkled. Although she had a pile of homework, she had yet to take her textbooks out of her bookbag. It was so much better to sit in her room, close her eyes, and think about Cassie.

Cassie didn't seem to have many friends. Sure, she hung out with the cheerleaders and student council members and the other popular kids—they lived in the same neighborhood of Tudors and palatial brick colonials; Esther had driven by a few times—but there was always something aloof about her. Esther doubted that she had a best friend. Some girls said that she was loose. Slutty. Esther figured those girls were just jealous. In spite of the scar, she was gorgeous. Maybe good looks were isolating. She wanted to be Cassie's friend, her confidante, her shoulder to cry on. And if anyone said anything bad about Cassie's scar or her alcoholic mother or her Daddy's skirt-chasing, well, Esther would punch them in the face. Just like she beat up that snot-nosed kid who picked on Harumi.

Esther remembered that day, remembered how the summer sun was frying the grass. She and Harumi were sitting on Esther's front porch, their feet on the hot concrete steps, waiting for the ice cream truck.

Cicadas buzzed in the bushes and Esther's little brother Mark wailed inside the house. Then, another sound—the tinkle of the big white van as it rounded the corner. Esther and Harumi had their quarters ready. Esther's was all slimy from sweat.

"What are you going to have today?" she asked.

Harumi looked into the sky and squinted at the sun. "I don't know. Maybe a grape Popsicle. But then I've got to go practice my violin."

Harumi was always practicing. Esther thought that her mother was cruel for making her practice all the time. Plus, Harumi was Esther's only friend and when she was busy studying Japanese or music or the abacus, there was no one else to play with.

"Here it comes." Harumi stood up and brushed off the back of her skirt. She waited till Esther had stood, and then led the way down the sidewalk.

The music tinkled like a wind-up toy, louder and louder, till the van was in full view. The vehicle came to a halt and a man in a white uniform and matching cap climbed out. All over the neighborhood, doors opened and kids spilled into the street. There were five or six of them pulling on the man's jacket and waving their money in the air.

Harumi and Esther approached slowly and solemnly. When they got to the van, they waited at the fringe until they were noticed.

"What'll it be, ladies?" The man was about the same age as Esther's father and his face was sprinkled with freckles.

The other kids, three boys and two girls, stood off to one side licking their fudge bars. They whispered among themselves and kicked at the pebbles in the road.

When the nice man in the white suit had taken their money, he doffed his cap at them and climbed back into the driver's seat. Soon the van was tinkling its way into another neighborhood.

Esther and Harumi turned and started to go back to the Shealy's yard.

"China girl," a falsetto voice chimed behind them. "Ain't no chop suey ice cream here. Why don't y'all go on home?"

Esther turned to see a boy slightly shorter than herself in a striped T-shirt and yellow shorts. He bit down on his lower lip, making buckteeth.

Harumi didn't look back. She kept her eyes on the ground and her feet in forward motion.

Although her friend didn't respond, Esther knew that she had heard the barbs and that they had lodged deep within her. But Harumi wasn't the type to scream and shout. She needed someone like Esther to defend her.

"She's not from China, you idiot," Esther shouted. "She's American."

"Then why do her mama and daddy talk so funny?"

"They came from Japan," Esther said. "They came here to be free."

He picked up a stone and tossed it at Harumi. It hit the back of her leg, but she didn't turn around. By now she was halfway to the Shealys' yard. She'd probably keep on going and run off to her own house. Then Esther would be alone for the rest of the day.

"I'll get you for that," Esther shrieked. She dropped her ice cream bar onto the pavement and ran straight for the little boy. When she got to him, she began pummeling him with her fists.

He fell onto the pavement, his fudge bar flying into the air. The other kids went running off in different directions.

Esther climbed onto the boy, pinning him to the ground, and yanked at his hair. Clumps of white-blond hair stuck to her sticky, sweaty hands. She tried to claw his hands away so she could spit on his face, but he kept his eyes and mouth shielded. By the time Esther's mother arrived, the boy was a sniveling mess.

Esther had gotten into big trouble, but she was still proud of her ferocity. Even now, she and Harumi would sometimes laugh about that day. Not that she saw Harumi much anymore.

Sometimes she invited Esther to go along to a party where she'd be playing with her new band, but Esther thought that she was just using her as an alibi. If her parents knew what she was doing on those Friday and Saturday nights (Not shopping at the mall! Not going to see movies at the Cineplex!) they'd probably chain her to her bedpost.

Harumi's life had changed. She and Esther were in different orbits.

5

Trudy's dad had once been in a band. He had photos and demo tapes to prove it. On one wall of his apartment there was a framed flyer advertising a riverside gig. They'd called themselves Swamp, after the mushy lowlands of South Carolina.

Trudy spent hours listening to Jack's tapes. Swamp's sound made her think of dusty roads and moonshine and cats in heat. They were a blues band, but sometimes they got happy, rollicking through their songs with the kick of rock and roll. Sometimes she grabbed a wooden spoon, held it like a mic, and sang along. One day, that would be her voice on tape.

Sarah had never told Trudy about the band. Maybe she didn't care or hadn't thought it was important. Sarah liked '60s Motown, after all, the sexy croon of Marvin Gaye, the bubbly optimism of the girl groups. Swamp's sound was something else.

Trudy tried to get to know Jack through his music while he was away at the university where he taught anthropology. Sometimes he brought his textbooks home and tried to interest her in the peoples of the world. She'd officially dropped out of school (she'd be coming into her trust fund in a couple of years and had no need of a diploma anyway), but he thought that he could teach her things. One night he prepared a slide show, there in the living room. They sat on the secondhand sofa with Cokes while Jack narrated.

Trudy looked at the images on the white wall and saw instead her father, holding a camera in a country far from her. Where had she been at that time? Curled up in the corner of her bedroom, evading Sarah's hysteria? Trying to keep her mother's boyfriend's hands out of her pants? She would have been happier in West Africa with her father, drums beating her to sleep at night.

Jack kept beer in the fridge and sometimes she'd crack open a can while watching the soaps. One afternoon she got carried away—two beers during *All My Children*, a couple more during *General Hospital*. Her dad found her still in her pajamas amid crumpled empties. He wasn't as mad as she'd expected. Sarah would have been furious. She'd have shipped Trudy off to a foster home like she had once before. That had been for slapping her little brother Joey. She didn't remember why she'd hit him, only a sense of never-ending fury that had finally made its way to her hand. Joey hadn't been injured, but he'd wailed like a banshee. Trudy had been sorry about it later, but she got sent away anyhow.

The foster family, the Andersons, had lived in an old house with a rotting porch. There were three other foster children as well. Trudy figured they were getting paid to take in the unwashed and unwanted because they hadn't seemed enthusiastic about parenting.

Mrs. Anderson sat in the den all day, a bowl of potato chips in her lap, watching game shows. Sometimes she asked Trudy to change the baby's diapers or run to the store for a pack of cigarettes. She was like their maid. She ran away five times.

Jack didn't send her to the Andersons or anywhere else. He had this liberal parent act going. Or maybe he didn't know that he was supposed to be strict.

"Trudy," he said calmly. He picked up one accordioned can and examined it. "First I'm going to go make us a pot of coffee. Then we're going to have a talk."

Trudy sat on the sofa, mute, too stunned for defiance. She grabbed a cushion and held it to her chest, rocked back and forth. He was probably going to beat her. Didn't Sarah say he'd given her a black eye once? But no. Trudy listened to him pulverize the beans in a hand-crank grinder. Then she heard the whistle of the kettle as the water came to a boil. Jack made coffee in a French press he'd gotten on one of his trips.

When he came back, he set down two mugs, opened the curtains, and sat on a stool in front of Trudy so they could talk face to face.

"I think you need something interesting to do," he said. "I'll give you a choice. You can help me at the university, or maybe we could find a job for you somewhere."

"I'll help you," she said, "at the university."

She went with him the next day even though she had a slight hangover. She wasn't used to drinking. The reform school had been dry, although some girls had managed to smuggle in some weed.

Trudy followed her father across campus, into the Humanities building where he had his office. She tried to keep her distance, not wanting to look like a kid tagging along. She wore lipstick and bright blue eye shadow.

Students were everywhere. Blankets decorated the lawn, and young men and women in cutoffs and tank tops sunned themselves. Frisbees sliced through the air. Music blasted from portable radios.

Jack led her to the elevator, then along a hallway to his office. She waited while he opened the door, looked both ways down the corridor as if planning her escape.

Jack's office was small and walled with books. His desk faced away from the window. There were a couple of straight-back chairs near the door for students. A beanbag chair took up one corner.

He showed her where the bathroom was and where she could get a drink of water. Then he led her back to the office. "Why don't you hang out here for a while? Read some books. Get a feel for the place." He left her there to go teach a class.

Trudy sat down in the swivel chair behind the desk. She pushed off against the desk and gave it a spin. When the chair came to a stop, she started looking in the drawers. Lots of pens, paper clips, a scattering of business cards. In the bottom drawer there were stacks of papers—drafts of an article Jack was working on. Something about Gullah coming-of-age rituals. And under that, last month's *Playboy*.

Trudy yanked it out, paged through and looked at the fleshpots. She studied Miss June's buxom figure. Trudy could copy that come-hither look, but how would she get those tits? Suddenly bored, she slammed the magazine down and got up from the chair. She was reading through the titles of books on the shelves when there was a knock on the door.

"Come in," she called out.

The door squeaked open and then, at first, only a head appeared. A guy, with short black spiky hair and eyeliner. His cheekbones jutted like cliffs over the hollow valleys of his cheeks.

"Is Dr. Baxter in?" His whole body came into view then—gangly limbs clothed in a shorn-sleeved T-shirt and black jeans. He had a chain—the kind you can buy by the yard at the hardware store—around his hips instead of a belt. His eyes followed Trudy. The black around them made him look like some young Egyptian prince.

"He's out," Trudy said. "I'm his assistant."

He cocked his head. Just then Trudy noticed the little dagger dangling from his right earlobe. "I didn't know he had an assistant. Are you a student here?"

"Uh, not exactly. Not this term."

"Cool. So what's your name? Mine's Adam, by the way."

"Adam. I'm Trudy." He was looking at her, sizing her up. She felt his gaze on her bleached blonde hair, her face, her uptilted breasts. "Hey, do you want to go get something to drink? I could use a break. It's kind of dull in here."

"Yeah, okay. I guess Dr. Baxter isn't coming back right away."

They went down to the snack bar and ordered Cokes. Trudy paid for her own. She'd filched a twenty from Jack's wallet the night before.

Adam told her that he was taking anthropology to fulfill a requirement, but he was really an art major.

"Cool," Trudy said. "What kind of stuff do you do?"

"Right now I'm making sculptures out of junk. I use coat hangers and hubcaps and bottles and whatever else I dig up. I have a piece called *Urban Bondage* that's pretty cool. You'd like it, I think."

Trudy was flattered. "You'll have to show it to me."

"Yeah, sure."

Trudy told him that she was seventeen and she had been in prison.

Adam didn't seem too alarmed. "What for?" he asked. "Were you a dealer?"

"Armed robbery," she lied. "My friend Lydia and I held up a 7-Eleven."

"With, like, a gun?"

"Yeah, but I don't have it anymore. The cops took it."

"I never met an ex-con before. Especially not a girl."

They talked for over an hour. Trudy tossed whatever she thought might interest him into the conversation. A trip to Benin. Her stint as a striptease artist. She was good at making stuff up.

Adam invited her to a party at his house that weekend. He and his housemates were going to get a couple of kegs and engage in an evening of debauchery.

She thought that debauchery sounded like fun.

Trudy arrived wearing a tight black dress without underwear.

The bash was already in full swing. People were draped over the porch railing and spilling onto the lawn. A few staggered in the street. Most of the partiers were college age, but Trudy saw some that looked younger than herself. Maybe they lived in the neighborhood.

She bypassed the keg and went in search of Adam. She had a mission and she was looking to complete it as soon as possible. She found him coming down a staircase.

"Hey," he said. "How's it going?" His eyes were red and she could tell he was stoned. Even so, he seemed aware enough to take in her dress and the body it contained.

"Show me your room," she blurted out. "I want to see your art."

"Right this way." He headed back up the stairs and Trudy followed.

He stopped at a closed door that had a sign reading Caution: Dangerous Chemicals hanging from the doorknob. Someone answered his knock and he shouted, "Hey, get the fuck out of there. This is my room."

Trudy stood waiting behind him in the hall till a rumpled-looking couple emerged.

"Enter," Adam said, motioning her inside.

Her foot came down on an empty pizza box. She wended her way through a maze of overflowing ashtrays and album covers and *Art in America* magazines. Half-finished sculptures crowded every corner. A mattress made an island in the middle of the room. Above the tousled sheets, a mobile hung from the ceiling—keys and spoons and can lids threaded onto fishing line.

He pulled her down onto the bed. Then his mouth was on hers, hard and searching, his tongue like a big sour slug. They wrestled out of their clothes, clashing teeth. Trudy thought that everything looked so much smoother in the movies.

It hurt like hell, but she didn't want him to know it was her first time. She moaned as if she were enjoying it. He rolled off her a few minutes later and reached into a drawer.

"I don't know about you, but I could sure use a joint."

All Trudy could think was, "I'm not a virgin anymore."

Everybody said it wasn't so great the first time. Trudy was willing to give it another shot. She liked knowing that when Adam was inside of her, she was the only thing on his mind. It made her feel important.

A month later, they were in Dr. Baxter's waterbed. This time was different. The motion of the waves rocked them, lulled them. Adam moved more cautiously, trying to gauge the movement of the liquid underneath.

"I love you," he said as he gathered her in his arms and nibbled at her neck.

Happiness bloomed in her, threatening to burst out of her chest. "Oh, I love you too, Adam." She dug her fingernails into his back, pulling him closer.

After it was over, they smoked some pot from Jack's stash, took a bath, and fell asleep. It was only three o'clock in the afternoon, but nothing could wake them—not the sound of a passing train, not the ringing of the telephone, not the opening and banging shut of the door.

"Trudy!" Only that—her name on her father's lips—could pull them out of their dreams. Then, "Adam!"

"Dad!"

"Dr. Baxter!"

"Get your clothes on. Now." He dragged them away from the scene of the crime to Goatfeathers, a coffee house down in Five Points, and all of his hippie cool disappeared. Suddenly he was a self-righteous square.

"Adam, do you realize how old my daughter is?"

"Sir, I didn't know she was your daughter."

Sir? Trudy could hardly believe her ears. What was going on here? Only a couple of hours before, he was telling her that he loved her, and now he was sucking up to her dad. Shouldn't he be defending her? Their relationship?

"She's fifteen."

"Sixteen," Trudy said. Her birthday was in a few days. What the hell difference did it make how old she was? Romeo and Juliet were fourteen. "And what I lack in years, I make up for in experience."

"That's enough, young lady." Jack's face was red. Trudy had made a fool of him. Clearly he wasn't used to this fatherhood business.

Trudy had seen it all before with each of her four stepfathers. They assumed the role, went as far as adopting her, asked her to call them "Dad." And then, as soon as Trudy did something they didn't like, there would be murmuring behind closed doors, ultimatums made. Sarah standing by, wringing her hands. Then announcements: She'd be going off to school/to stay with distant relatives/to the juvie home.

Trudy slouched back in the booth. She'd expected more from Adam, at least. But he just sat there, avoiding her eyes. She took a toothpick out of the faux-crystal holder and stabbed it into the tip of her index finger, trying to make the pain in her body match the aching in her heart. The wood didn't puncture skin. Jack saw what she was doing and grabbed her hand.

"You'd better know that this could get us all in trouble. Trudy is a minor. You know what that means, don't you?"

Trudy held her gaze steady on Adam. She willed him to look over at her so she could roll her eyes at "Dr. Baxter's" paranoia. He didn't really care about her, Trudy. He was only concerned with his precious career. No wonder Sarah had left him.

But Adam would not look her way. She felt like that woman with the snakes growing from her head—Medusa. Was he afraid he'd turn to stone or something? She found his foot under the table with her own and nudged his ankle. She needed a sign from him, some indication that he was still on her side, but he jerked away. The future of their romance was looking pretty bleak.

Jack stepped away and gave them a few minutes of privacy.

"Well, I guess this is it," Adam said. "See you around."

"What are you talking about?" Trudy's voice was shrill with desperation. "You really care what he thinks?"

"Hey, I need to graduate." His kohl-lined eyes were strangely cold. He eased himself out of the booth and headed for the door.

When Adam was gone, Jack ordered two more cups of coffee. "I'm sorry Trudy," he said, "but I'm afraid we're going to have to make other arrangements."

6

Cassie knew that rumors about her were flourishing at school. Todd's football buddies snickered in her wake. Their girlfriends darted their eyes from Cassie to each other and whispered behind their hands.

October, November, December . . . Cassie ticked off the months in her head. She couldn't wait to get out of there.

Todd must have been pretty angry when she ditched him at that party, but he was the one slobbering all over Miss Big Blonde. She'd had every right to leave.

But Todd wasn't used to indifferent dates. He probably couldn't believe that Cassie, a girl with a disfiguring scar, wouldn't jump through hoops to be his girlfriend. This was his way of getting back at her.

She passed Harumi on her way to American Lit. When Harumi saw her, the usual chill left her eyes and she smiled.

"Hey, Cassie. How's it going?"

"Thanks again for the ride the other night."

"Sure. Anytime."

After they'd ditched the party, they'd wound up going to the Capitol Café downtown. A waitress named Pee Wee brought them coffee and scrambled eggs, and they'd compared notes on stage mothers, itchy costumes, and favorite songs. They'd even hatched plans to perform together someday. Harumi was sick of her bandmates and ready for something more serious. Maybe Cassie would be interested in being the lead singer?

Later, they'd gone across the street and wandered around the capitol grounds, under the palmetto trees, past the spotlit monuments dedicated to George Washington and the Confederate soldiers, talking and talking until nearly dawn.

They'd have to make plans to hang out together again soon, Cassie thought as she made her way to class. For now, she sat down at her desk, hauled out her textbook, and waited for the bell to ring.

It had to be hard for Harumi, being a minority, she thought. And her life was so different from everyone else's. Instead of going to volleyball or cheerleader practice after school, or even kicking back in front of MTV at home, Harumi had gone off to play her violin. She'd never dated, as far as Cassie knew. Harumi hadn't said anything about boys the other night. Maybe the guys at their school didn't want to go out with someone of another race—especially the ones with the Confederate flag decals on their car windows. Or maybe they were intimidated by that angry aura that surrounded her. It could have been something else. She might have a boyfriend at another school—a college poet or a pianist. A secret lover.

The bell rang and Ms. Claiborne shuffled into class. Speaking of outsiders, she was pretty much one herself. Today she was wearing an all-black outfit—a turtleneck that clung to her bony chest, a miniskirt revealing stick-like legs, and a black beret, slightly askew, which hid most of her short auburn hair. Her lipstick was white.

Ms. Claiborne always dressed eccentrically for a high school English teacher, but the beret was a special addition meant to evoke a bygone era of coffee houses and beatniks. Ms. Claiborne had hung out in Greenwich Village in the '60s. Rumor had it she'd once smoked pot with Jack Kerouac.

"Now, you've all memorized your selections," she said hopefully. "You're all ready for today's poetry reading, aren't you?"

"We need clove cigarettes," someone heckled from the back row.

A wave of giggles passed through the room. Ms. Claiborne smiled patiently. She waited till silence returned, then scanned the upturned faces. "Well? Who's first?"

Rusty Andrews raised his hand. Cassie had been out with him a few times her junior year. Like Todd, he was a BMOC coasting on looks and easy charm. In another ten years, he'd be balding and fat from beer. Cassie could see the signs already.

He scooted his chair back, rose from his seat, and strode to the head of the classroom. Then he cracked his neck and cleared his throat loudly.

Titters erupted.

Cassie checked out Ms. Claiborne's expression. Her chalky lips were pressed together. She didn't have much tolerance for those who lacked the proper respect for literature.

Rusty saw her face and subdued his smirk. He began his recitation: "Hickory dickory dock . . . ."

Wild laughter broke out.

Ms. Claiborne had asked the students to memorize their favorite poems. In the spirit of the '60s, she'd given them total freedom in choosing what they would recite. They were allowed—encouraged, even—to go beyond *The Norton Anthology of American Literature* and dig up poems from obscure literary journals and hip small presses. Mother Goose wasn't exactly what she'd had in mind, and everyone knew it. Rusty would probably get a D on this assignment. A C, if he was lucky. After all, he hadn't flubbed the lines.

"That was very entertaining, Mr. Andrews," Ms. Claiborne said once he'd returned to his seat. He was slapping the palms of his neighboring students. "I'm glad to see that you're still in touch with your inner child. Anyone else have a favorite nursery rhyme?"

After a long pause, Cassie raised her hand.

A strange hush fell over the room and she was reminded of the mysterious rumor floating around the halls. Her audience sat with crossed arms and blank faces. Cassie was surprised that they were listening at all. "'Lady Lazarus,' by Sylvia Plath," she said, naming her selection. Then she began her performance.

"*I have done it again,*" she recited. She told the class about dying and coming back to life. She became Lady Lazarus. The classroom was silent, except for her voice, the enchantment complete.

"*Dying / Is an art, like everything else.*" She paused. "*I do it exceptionally well.*"

They were all listening.

"*For the eyeing of my scars, there is a charge.*" She touched the crescent on her cheek. "*For the hearing of my heart— / It really goes.*" Here, she thumped her chest with her palm.

Ms. Claiborne, propped on the edge of her desk, had put down her pen as if she'd forgotten that this was a graded exercise.

By the time Cassie got to the last part, about rising out of the ash with red hair, she knew that she would be getting an A. Performing like this was electrifying. *Powerful.* How could she have forgotten how wonderful it felt? She delivered the final words with a snarl: "*And I eat men like air.*"

Rusty Andrews squirmed in his seat. Cassie glared at him, cast her gaze over all of the students, and then returned to her desk. Silence fell heavily.

Finally Ms. Claiborne thawed and took a deep breath. "Wow. You are quite an actress. That was most impressive."

Cassie smiled. "Thank you." She knew that word would spread quickly. She would be officially weird, but she didn't care. There was so much beyond high school. She was ready to burn her bridges and move into the world.

7

Trudy had been to The Cave a few times with Adam. She thought of it as their place, and every time she climbed that narrow staircase, she expected to see him. The club was on the second floor of a run-down building on Assembly Street, next to a row of pawnshops. There was a parking garage across the street. During the day, looking up from the street, it looked like the kind of place where nothing would ever happen, but at night, the doors opened and the hall rumbled with pounding combat boots. Music blasted from a loft in the corner.

Everyone danced solo, writhing as if they were in pain. Trudy understood. She threw herself into their midst, a whirling dervish, a tornado, a woman scorned.

When she was tired of dancing, she slunk back into the Pink Room, a lounge with thrift shop sofas. The walls were hung with splatter paintings.

One night, Trudy stumbled into the Pink Room and found something new: a dented birdcage with a ratty-haired Barbie doll hanging inside. A chain—the kind attached to bathtub plugs—was wrapped around her neck and rigged to the top of the cage. The doll was naked and its plastic flesh nicked as if by a razor blade. On the bottom of the cage there was a scattering of newspaper clippings. Trudy leaned in closer and saw that they were all concerned with sex scandals. A priest and a boy. A kindergarten teacher and a child porno ring. A Boy Scout troop leader who exposed himself to passing teenaged girls. There was an index card taped to the wall behind the cage: "*Jail Bait* by Adam Walker."

Someone came up behind her. "I think it's offensive, don't you?" Trudy turned to see a young woman with an inch of black hair all over her head. She was wearing jeans with suspenders over a T-shirt. Her feet were encased in Doc Martens. "He must hate women."

"No," Trudy said. "You don't understand. He's my boyfriend. He's in love with me. I'm, like, his muse."

The young woman looked at her strangely. "Wake up, girl. That Barbie doll has been lynched."

Trudy was sure that the noose meant something else. Thwarted desire. Strangled hopes. She rode her bike to Adam's apartment at least once a day. Sometimes one of his roommates answered. Always the same response: "He's not here, Trudy. I don't know when he'll be back."

But one day, she forced herself into the room beyond.

"Wait—"

Dave stepped up to the doorway. "I don't think Adam is going to be too happy to find you here." He pulled at his hair.

Trudy glared at him. "Leave me alone."

Dave shifted from side to side, looked toward the screen door, then threw up his hands. "Don't say I didn't warn you."

Trudy slammed the door in his face. This was her room as much as any other room in her life had been. She knew where everything was—the condoms in the drawer, Adam's secret stash, the rolling papers. She flipped on the stereo and picked out an album. Then she slipped off her clothes, rolled herself a joint, and wrapped herself in sheets to wait.

She heard the front door hinges screech about an hour later, then a slam and the tom-tom pound of footsteps. She lay against the pillows while she listened to the low rumble of voices in the room beyond. Then, a curse, a bang against the wall, the door thrown open, Adam yanking her by the arm with such force her shoulder popped out of joint. She was too stoned to feel much pain. "Adam . . . I love what you did for me . . . the birdcage . . . the doll."

Trudy thought she could see little licks of flame in Adam's eyes. Behind him, Dave turned from her nakedness. There was someone else in the room. Female. Long rusty hair.

"Trudy, we're through. Get out of here."

"I'm homeless, Adam. He kicked me out. Have a heart."

His grip on her arm loosened. A dozen emotions flickered across his face. "I don't believe you," he said at last. "You lie about everything."

"It's true," she said. "I swear. You can call him. He threw my ass on the street."

He let go of her then and she reeled back.

"Get dressed," he said. He left her alone and closed the door behind him.

Trudy started crying. She crawled back under the covers and her mascara-tinged tears smudged the pillow. She heard the door creak and slam again and then she jumped out of bed again, a wild woman. He wasn't coming back. He'd gone off with that wench. She wanted to hurt him somehow, to make him feel as wretched as she felt then, naked and abandoned. There was a rolled-up sketch standing at the foot of the bed. She lit a match and set it on fire.

8

Esther took a deep breath and followed Harumi into the apartment. Harumi had said "party" and "college." Although Esther was nervous about the whole thing, she was tired of staying at home, always the uninvited one, while her brother Mark went to bash after bash. If nothing else, she told herself, she'd have a chance to work on her social skills. She was grateful to Harumi for asking her along. And although they hadn't been all that close lately, she was glad that they were still friends. She'd missed Harumi.

This wasn't the usual party where all the breakables and valuables were locked up in the master bedroom so Mom and Dad wouldn't get upset when they got home from their cruise. The thrift shop furniture was already wrecked.

"Is there anybody that I know here?" Esther asked, hovering a little too close to Harumi.

"There's me." Harumi was messing with her bass, too distracted to give Esther much attention. "Look, you said you wanted to come. Get in line at the keg. Mingle."

Esther was hurt, but tried to hide it. Somehow, she'd thought that they'd be hanging out together. "Okay. Have a great show."

Harumi rolled her eyes. "Yeah, right. This is show biz, all the way."

Ever since her audition at Juilliard, she'd been a bit harder, a bit colder. Esther wished she'd just talk about it, but Harumi never brought up New York or her violin. She probably thought that Esther, who'd never been north of Virginia, or a master of anything, was incapable of understanding. Maybe in time Harumi would go back to being her old self.

If only Esther could play a musical instrument. Then Harumi would think of her as more of an equal. They could even be in a band together. Maybe Esther could be a backup singer, or a songwriter. She could learn to play the guitar! Yeah, right.

Esther worked up a smile and found her way to the bathroom where the keg was chilling in the tub. "Hi," she said to a tall guy with a black T-shirt and squiggly hair. He winked and moved on. Esther pretended that she belonged there and that she was comfortable.

No one spoke to her while she waited in line to get a plastic cup filled with beer. They all seemed to know each other. Across the room, she spotted a thin woman with bleached butch-cut hair. She was leaning against the wall, hip cocked, like a model in *Vogue*. Why couldn't Esther look like that? Tall and thin and exotically beautiful.

The woman caught her staring and raised her drink in a toast.

Esther looked away quickly, embarrassed. She felt odd with her ordinary reddish-brown shoulder-length hair and her plain face. She wished that she had dabbed on some lipstick, at least. And maybe she should have worn something other than jeans and a flannel shirt. These women were like tropical birds, dazzling and rare in their finery. Esther looked like a roadie for the third-rate garage band warming up.

"Hey there, dear. You look lost."

The British accent jarred Esther out of her gloom. She improvised a smile for the model-thin woman with white hair, now standing before her. Her cotton dress was so tight that Esther could see her nipples. She obviously wasn't wearing a bra.

"I'm Rebecca," she said, holding out a hand.

"Esther." Rebecca's hand was bony and cool.

"Did you crash the wrong party, darling? You look a little muddled."

Esther's back stiffened. "I'm here with my friend, Harumi. The band, I mean."

"Ahh." Rebecca's thin penciled eyebrows rose. "So you're in high school."

"Well, yeah. I'm a senior."

"Ahh."

Esther had finally reached the bathtub. The most gorgeous guy she had ever seen was now pumping beer into her cup. He was wearing cut-offs, no shirt, and even though it was October, he was amazingly tanned. His belly was taut and segmented.

"There you go," he said. For a split second, she had the pleasure of looking into those chocolate eyes, half-hidden by the wavy hair that fell to his chin.

"Thanks." She wanted to talk more, but he had already forgotten her, his attention on the next cup.

Esther moved out of line, a little shaken by her brush with beauty. Rebecca was still there, watching her with an amused twist of the lips.

"You can't have him," she whispered, pulling Esther out of hearing.

"What?"

Rebecca ushered her onto the balcony where a few people were smoking and talking. "That's Tony," she said, nodding her head toward the keg. "You can't have him. Don't waste your energy."

Esther blushed. She hadn't been thinking of making a play. Someone like that was obviously beyond her grasp. She'd never presume to want him. He was just nice to look at, like a statue of David or something.

Rebecca was staring at her, watching her every reaction. "You can't have him, Esther, because he's gay."

"What?" Esther had never met an openly gay person before. Sure, there was talk about certain kids at school, such as Lewis Dalton who'd once been spotted purchasing needlepoint supplies. Everyone knew, but he was still in the closet.

"Are all of these guys . . . gay?" Esther asked. She couldn't imagine the straight boys at school drinking alongside a self-declared queer.

"No, but some are," Rebecca said. "Some of the women, too."

Esther turned and looked at her then, a little frightened. "Are you?"

"What if I am?"

Esther didn't reply. Her head was suddenly too light, as if it were about to drift from her shoulders into the starry sky. She could smell Rebecca's perfume. She could feel the heat of her body.

Rebecca lowered her voice. "What if I told you that I think you're really beautiful and I want to kiss you?"

Esther brought her beer to her lips and drank like a horse in the desert. She set her empty cup on the railing. "Do you think I'm gay?" she whispered.

"There's just something about you that I really like."

Esther wondered what it would be like to kiss this woman. What would her lipstick taste like? What would it be like to run her fingers over Rebecca's ribs, her back, her pea-sized nipples? What would it be like to be kissed in return?

When Rebecca took her hand and pulled her back into the living room, she didn't resist. She followed her to the tub and got her cup refilled. She drank and drank, and then she didn't care when Rebecca led her into a dark room and nudged her onto the bed. She closed her eyes and felt Rebecca's lips brushing hers. A shiver went down her spine. And then the light came on and she looked to see Harumi standing in the doorway.

Her face was totally expressionless, but Esther knew that wild thoughts roiled underneath. "I'm leaving now," she said in a frosty voice. "Are you coming or not?"

Esther nodded. She couldn't speak. This was the most embarrassing moment of her life. When Harumi left the room, she looked toward the window, seriously considering jumping. Everyone would stare knowingly when she emerged from the room.

They probably knew that Rebecca was queer and that the two of them had gone off together. She might as well commit suicide right now.

"Sorry about that, luv," Rebecca said, still lolling on the bed. "I should have put a chair under the doorknob or something."

Esther didn't answer. She heaved herself off the bed and smoothed out her clothes. The room was spinning. Behind her, Rebecca was scrabbling through the drawers of the nightstand. When she turned, Esther could see that she was writing something.

Rebecca prowled across the room and draped her arm over Esther's shoulder. "Here's my phone number, darling," she whispered, tucking a folded piece of paper in Esther's shirt pocket. "Call me."

Esther felt Rebecca's lips on her neck before the other woman moved away. She crawled under the covers and closed her eyes. Esther tucked in her shirt, turned off the light, and went to find Harumi.

All the way home, they sat in total silence. Harumi didn't even turn the radio on. Maybe she was sick of music for the night. Maybe she was waiting for Esther to explain. But she couldn't. What had happened had been beyond her control. It was as if Rebecca had hypnotized her. Well, actually she'd been drunk. And it hadn't been bad. It had been really, really nice. No one had ever told Esther that she was beautiful or desired. And no one had ever kissed her like that. What was so wrong with it? Of course she wouldn't call Rebecca. No, she'd wad up that little piece of paper and put her out of her mind. Someday it would seem like a dream.

When the car reached Esther's house, Harumi parked at the curb. She stared straight ahead and waited.

"Thanks," Esther said. "For the ride, I mean. And for taking me with you."

Harumi acted as if she hadn't heard. She kept her eyes on the windshield until Esther had slammed the door and run across the yard to the front porch of her house. Then she drove home, two blocks away.

Esther wasn't sure what would happen next. Part of her was afraid that Harumi and her fellow band members would broadcast her little adventure all over school. She'd be ostracized, maybe tarred and feathered. People would paint rude slogans on her locker. Call her a dyke.

But it wasn't like that at all. Everyone treated her the same as before, except for Harumi who acted as if she didn't exist. If their eyes happened to meet in the hallway, Harumi looked right through her.

It was weird. They'd played together all through childhood, spending the night at each other's houses in each other's beds. And then suddenly, nothing. Esther had never been so lonely in her life.

At night, she cried herself to sleep. Then she had dreams—vivid erotic dreams—about Rebecca. Or sometimes she dreamed of Cassie, of licking her scar and wrapping her in yards of pink silk. She was haunted by all the wrong things. Maybe some kind of exorcism was in order. A visit to a shrink. But how could she bring this up with her parents? This kind of problem didn't appear in *Good Housekeeping* or *Family Circle* or the other magazines her mother read. Whenever her father saw a guy with an earring, he muttered "homo." She was alone.

9

When Jack threatened to send Trudy back to Sarah, she lit out on her own. She was living now in a rented house. Every month her grandparents sent her a check for eight hundred dollars to cover living expenses. She wouldn't come into her trust fund until she turned twenty-one, but her Charleston grandmother had taken pity on her. She didn't want the girl eating out of garbage cans.

Trudy's room was at the back of the house, off the kitchen. At the moment, the sink was filled with a week's worth of dirty dishes, some of them furred with grey. Trudy tried to mask the odor by burning incense.

She was stuck with a slob—Madeline—but at least she had her own room. She had a futon in the corner and a few milk crates for her books and candles.

She'd met her apartment-mate at The Cave. In between slamming and dancing and taking turns in the DJ booth, Trudy took breaks in the Pink Room and became intimately acquainted with the clientele. She'd decided to start a band.

Trudy got her hands on a guitar. Actually, it was her father's guitar, the one he'd played back in the day, with Swamp. The instrument had a history of smoky bars, fields of wildflowers, park benches, Greyhound buses. It had been all over the place, probably even Dahomey.

She was going to ask to borrow it, but when she dropped by Jack's apartment, he wasn't home. Trudy decided to cart the guitar off anyhow. He never played it anymore and besides, he might say no if she asked him to loan it to her. He didn't trust her so much since all the trouble with Adam.

She'd practice and innovate and turn herself into a brilliant performer. And then she'd start a band. It would be the most exciting thing to hit the town since General Sherman. Yeah, these were good thoughts.

By day, she practiced. By night, she hung out at The Cave, playing records or slamming on the dance floor. During breaks, she looked for musicians in the Pink Room.

"Hey, Maddy. I'm starting a band. Wanna join up?"

Madeline tossed a lock of black hair out of her eyes. "You must be out of your mind."

Trudy shrugged. She asked Jeff, the David Bowie lookalike. She even asked Johnny Fad. People laughed, blew smoke in her face. Sometimes they just turned away as if they hadn't heard her at all.

Why did everyone treat her proposition like some sort of joke? She was as serious as she'd ever been. The more she practiced, the more she knew that her dreams lay in music. She closed her eyes and saw herself on the stage, crooning into a mic while a huge crowd lit and lofted their Bics in tribute.

When people were drinking and dancing, they weren't in the mood for serious talk. She had to find another way to put her band together.

Trudy made a flyer with scissors and magazines and Elmer's glue. When she was finally satisfied with her work, she rode her housemate's rickety bicycle to Kinko's and made a hundred copies. Then she ran around Five Points, where all the college kids hung out, and plastered them to every telephone pole in sight with a staple gun. When she was finished, she went back to the apartment, picked up her guitar, and waited for the phone to ring.

"Hey, what's this?" Madeline barged into her room just after midnight, smelling of booze and smoke. She waved one of Trudy's flyers in the air between them.

"I'm starting a band," Trudy said. "I told you already."

Madeline shrugged. "Yeah, whatever. I wish you hadn't put our phone number down, though. We'll get half a million calls from creeps."

Trudy didn't answer. Why was Madeline being such a bitch? She looked really cool with her tattooed shoulder and asymmetrical haircut, but sometimes she could be totally square.

"I'll get my dad to buy us an answering machine," Trudy said. "That way we can screen calls."

Madeline nodded, seemingly consoled, and wandered off to her room.

Trudy giggled softly. Jack would never fork out cash for something like that, but the lie had worked.

The first call came at noon the next day.

"Hey, I'm calling about the band," a gravelly voice said.

"What do you play?"

"Bass, drums, whatever. I'm versatile. Hey, wait. You sound really familiar. What's your name?"

"Trudy B." She was trying out different names. "Baxter" sounded so boring.

"Hey, I know you. You're that psycho jailbird." The line went dead.

Later, Southern Bell called about an overdue phone bill. The manager at Yesterday's, where Madeline waited tables, called asking Madeline to report to work early. Someone dialed a wrong number.

Where were all the budding musicians, the soulmates in tune with her dreams? Trudy set aside her guitar and put on some music. She threw herself on the bed and let Patti Smith comfort her.

How was she ever going to get this thing off the ground? Trudy sighed. Maybe she could go solo—set up a drum machine and play the guitar herself. She wracked her brains trying to come up with someone who'd gotten famous without backup. Her mind went blank.

Two nights later, when she came home from a trip to the Quick Mart down the street, Madeline greeted her with, "You got a phone call. Someone wants to join your band."

"Great." Trudy felt like pogoing. "Who?" She pictured a pale, black-haired guy in leather, a guitar strapped across his hard-muscled body.

"I don't know. She said she'd call back."

She? *Well, okay. This could be good. A girl group. Yeah, that's the ticket.* They'd be like the Supremes with instruments. The Go-Go's with attitude. It would be a good gimmick, something to get them started while they developed as a band.

"You know, Madeline, you can still get in on the ground floor," Trudy teased happily. "I think you've got what it takes to be a first class drummer." She reached over and squeezed her housemate's biceps. Her muscles were hard from carrying trays of beer mugs and beef burritos.

The phone trilled and Trudy dove for it. She snatched the receiver on the second ring. "Yeah?"

"Hi, I'm, um, calling about the band?"

Trudy gave Madeline the thumbs up sign. Madeline rolled her eyes and retreated to her bedroom.

"Do you play an instrument?"

"No, but I can learn. I took piano lessons, so I can read music and I sing. I've written some songs, too."

Trudy didn't have much use for a piano, but keyboards—yeah, maybe. Anyway, this chick had a musical background. Her phone voice wasn't bad. She could probably sing backup.

"Cool. Why don't we meet and discuss this?"

"Um, okay."

"What's your name, by the way?"

"Cassandra Haywood. Cassie, for short."

Cassie? Trudy groaned inwardly. She'd seen her before at The Cave. Cassie, the poseur who looked like Barbie, but pretended to be a punk. She was blonde and whenever she took the dance floor, guys orbited her like planets. Trudy figured that she was stupid. She was slumming. She probably lived in a nice home with a pool and wore real pearls when she went out to dinner. The girl probably wrote songs about dressing up for dates and broken fingernails. Her image was totally wrong for what Trudy had in mind. Then again, it wasn't as if the phone had been ringing off the hook. And Trudy wasn't wild about the idea of a solo career.

"Let's meet at Group Therapy tomorrow," she said, naming a popular bar in Five Points.

"Okay, Trudy. I'll see you then."

As Trudy sat in her room that night, picking out chords on her guitar, she thought about Cassie. Maybe it wouldn't be so bad having her in the band. In spite of her scar, she was pretty in an obvious way, a way that men liked. Maybe her good looks would help them to draw a crowd.

Okay. They'd try it. Trudy knew about band histories—the breakups and rearrangements that went with the territory. If Cassie flopped, Trudy would kick her out of the group. In the meantime, her options weren't exactly multiplying.

Trudy flashed her fake ID at the door and shoved her way through to the back. Cassie was already there, alone in a booth, sipping what looked like Coke. Trudy slid into the seat across from her.

"So what do you want to do in the band?" Trudy asked.

"Whatever you want." Cassie reached behind her and pulled a notebook out of her backpack. She handed it to Trudy. "These are some songs I've written."

Cassie's scrawl filled up half the pages.

At first, Trudy just skimmed over the titles—"Crash Baby," "Pretty Please," "Lady Lazarus Rises Again," "Daddy's Disease." Then she went to the lyrics. Cassie, she realized, was not what she seemed. In spite of her all-American good looks—those blue eyes and that tumble of wheat-colored hair, her size eight physique—inside she was deeply warped.

Close up like this, Trudy could see the sickle-shaped scar that bisected her cheek. Usually, in the dark, it was barely visible. Trudy had always wondered about it, but never asked. Now she did. "How'd you get that scar?"

Cassie's hand flew to her face and covered the mark. It was almost a reflex, Trudy thought.

"Car accident," Cassie said. "I lived. Mama died."

And then, as if the words had been waiting to come out of her for years, Cassie's story began to flow. She told Trudy about the child beauty pageants, her mother's drinking, her father's affairs.

"The night my mama died, she was yelling at Daddy about bringing home some disease. I didn't realize it then, but now I know that he gave her herpes or something." Cassie shook her head in disgust.

Trudy wasn't sure which was worse—a dead mother, or a living mother who didn't give a damn. She told Cassie about her own sordid upbringing, about the time she'd spent locked up. Most people got all wide-eyed when they heard her biography, but Cassie took it all in with occasional nods and murmurs. Her own tragedies had left her shell-shocked. She was beyond surprise.

Later, they went back to Trudy's house and jammed with the guitar.

"Okay, you sing or scream or whatever, and I'll play," Trudy said. She sat on her bed, the guitar in her arms. As soon as her fingers touched the strings, Cassie began flailing like a spastic rag doll.

"*This is number one. I did it with a gun. This is number two. I made myself turn blue. This is number three. I drove into a tree. This is number four. I dove from the top floor. Lady Lazarus! I'm Lady Lazarus!*"

The girl had presence, no doubt about it. Trudy felt hope swell in her chest. They were going to be legends. They'd be a force to reckon with, an inspiration for every little girl in America—hell, the world!

Cassie finished her number and fell onto the bed. Her perfect breasts rose and fell with each deep breath. "I feel alive right now," she said, smiling at the ceiling. "*Really* alive."

"Yeah, I think this might work. You and me and . . . ."

Cassie sat up as if sparked by an idea. "I know this great bass player. She's a true musician—a child prodigy—and she's really cool. I'll bet she'd be interested. I could ask her."

Trudy nodded. Everything was coming together now. She couldn't believe she had ever been worried. "We'll have our first practice here on Friday night. Get her to come then."

It was already midnight. Madeline banged on the door. "Stop the racket. Y'all sound like a bunch of screaming divas," she said in a weary voice. "I'm going to bed now."

Trudy yanked open the door. "Maddy! I've got a band now. Tell the world."

Madeline slouched there in an oversized T-shirt, her face scrubbed clean. She didn't move when Trudy grabbed her and kissed her on the cheek. "You can still join. We need a drummer."

Madeline patted her on the head and disappeared into her room.

"An enemy of rock and roll," Trudy whispered to Cassie. "But we'll convert her."

That night, the two of them shared a bed. It was kind of nice watching Cassie's face relax into innocence and feeling the warmth of her body. This could be an initiation rite—sleeping together in the same bed. Anyone who hogged the sheets would be kicked out of the band.

10

Esther hadn't been planning on calling Rebecca. In fact, she shredded and burned the scribbled phone number as she'd promised herself in the car. But one Saturday afternoon, while shopping at the Columbia Mall for her mother's birthday gift, she caught a glimpse of her. At first, she wasn't sure. A tall woman with cropped white-blonde hair stood at the Lancôme makeup counter, bent over an array of creams. Esther could only see the back of her—the long, slender but shapely legs, the slightly rounded bottom bound in a tight, black skirt. And then the woman picked up a tube of lipstick and tilted the mirror on the counter. Esther saw her face.

She could have run in the other direction without being seen, but when she knew it was Rebecca, something leapt inside of her. Buoyed, but also suddenly shy, Esther moved slowly across the store.

"Hey," she said, priming herself for rejection.

Rebecca's eyes widened in the mirror. She smiled. "Esther!"

And then they'd wound up going out for coffee, and although Esther had tried to make small talk she'd wound up crying and telling Rebecca about her estrangement from Harumi and all the unfamiliar feelings that had been flooding her heart and mind. But she didn't tell her how she felt about Cassie. She wanted to keep that to herself.

In the daylight, in that black skirt and blazer, with her makeup just so, Rebecca looked professional. She listened attentively, looking away only to stir sugar in her coffee, and made little cooing noises whenever Esther paused. It was easy to imagine that she was talking to a counselor or an older and wiser sister.

"My parents were really conservative," Rebecca said. "If they'd known I was having feelings for my year nine teacher, they probably would have sent me off to some re-education camp." She shook her head and the thick gold hoops looped through her ears flashed with light. "Your friend will come around," she said. "And if she doesn't? Well, that'll be her loss."

They talked and talked, and Esther forgot all about buying a present for her mother. She drank three cups of coffee while Rebecca told her story. Her parents had kicked her out of the house when she'd declared her love for women, and after a few difficult years in London, stripping and selling drugs, she'd made her way to more tolerant shores. Now she was living in Columbia, selling art in one of the galleries in Five Points.

"You're the only one I've ever been able to talk to about this," Esther told her. And then she confessed to having ripped up Rebecca's telephone number.

Rebecca smiled kindly. "I came on a little strong that night, didn't I? I didn't mean to scare you. Then again, a jolt like that might have done you some good." She took a gold-plated pen out of her purse and wrote the number on a napkin. "If you ever want to talk—even if it's the middle of the night—call me."

Rebecca gave Esther a part-time job in her gallery. It was only after school and on weekends, and the money wasn't great, but Esther loved the atmosphere. Even when hours went by with no customers, she loved sitting on a stool behind the counter, sipping café au lait and looking at the paintings. There were a few tableaus of gardens and historic houses for the tourists, along with an oil painting or two of hunting dogs. But there were also edgy abstract compositions and surreal juxtapositions of zebras and belles.

Esther loved meeting the artists who sometimes came by to drop off a new painting or pick up a check. She'd met Blue Sky, whose most famous mural was featured in the *World Book Encyclopedia* under "Art." She also liked meeting up-and-coming artists like that guy Adam, who'd waltzed in the other day with his sculptures made out of junk. Rebecca had been impressed.

Rebecca was teaching Esther all about art, and all about how to style herself. Under the older woman's guidance, Esther had transformed herself from frump to Gypsy Queen. These days she wore her hair loosely rippled over her shoulders and she'd started wearing ethnic dresses with lots of beads. She wore makeup, too, but only when she was at the gallery. At school, she preferred to fade into the woodwork.

Now Esther had this double life. She was part of the hip Five Points scene in one life, and a lovelorn high school student in another. The lovelorn student pined for a girl she could never have. She wrote letters to Cassie and left them unsigned. She fed them into the mailbox at the corner. Of course there was never a reply.

11

From the DJ loft, Trudy looked down upon her kingdom. As long as she spun the discs, she was ruler of the dance floor. Right now, "Bela Lugosi's Dead" echoed against the brick walls, haunting the dancers. They staggered like atomic blast survivors, swooped over the floor like vampires.

Midway through the song, Jan hauled himself up the ladder leading to the booth. He motioned Trudy to approach him.

"The band will be coming on after this, so you can come down now," he said.

He paid her under the table for playing records at the club a few nights a week. That and the monthly checks from her grandmother were enough to live on. Or would have been if she spent her money wisely. She was crazy with cash. She bought records and music magazines and clothes. She spent way too much money on pot.

"Okay if I watch from up here?" Sometimes it was nice to groove in her own little world, to fall into the music without someone slamming her across the floor.

Jan shrugged. "Yeah, whatever."

He climbed down the ladder and, staying close to the wall, made his way back behind the bar.

Trudy sank back into the music, spellbound by Peter Murphy's voice.

Tonight's band was new. They'd performed a couple of times already—at parties and at a larger twenty-one-and-over club across town. Rumor had it that they were good enough for Atlanta, good enough even to attract sniffs from big city talent scouts. Columbia could be the next big scene.

The song ended. Trudy turned away from the dance floor, took the record off the turntable, and slid it into its sleeve. Down below, the dancers cleared the floor and the band fiddled around onstage with speakers and wires and instruments.

The club had become Trudy's life. She arrived almost as soon as it opened and stayed till it closed. She knew all the regulars like Johnny Fad, who pretended to be in love with Cassie, even though he was gay, and Jeff, the David Bowie lookalike who was a fry cook by day, but a mysterious object of allure by night as he sat at the bar in a black hat like a South American cowboy might wear. Trudy loved talking to him. Their conversations were peppered with allusions to Marguerite Duras films, Baudelaire, and Jim Carroll. Jeff was going to be a writer and Trudy felt sure she'd be a character in one of his books.

Then there was Keith, who always wore a black leather motorcycle jacket, and spoke in a whisper. He was an artist. He painted icons like James Dean and Jackie O, which Trudy thought was cool, but she was pretty sure her heart couldn't take another tortured artist. She wanted a musician.

The band was onstage now—three guys and a young woman with long straw-colored hair. She had a guitar slung across her body. Trudy could see that she was barefoot. A granny dress swept against her ankles.

Trudy felt a flash of envy whenever she saw a girl in a group. Girls stood out because they were so rarely in local bands. Everyone noticed them. Up in the DJ loft, Trudy was like a phantom. She wanted to be onstage, sucking up the energy of the crowd. And she would be, as soon as she and Cassie found a couple more members to round out their band.

"Hey." The lead singer stepped up to the mic. His red hair blazed in the lights. Round tinted glasses hid his eyes. He was tall and thin and androgynous. Trudy leaned over the side of the loft to be closer to him. "I'm Noel," he said. "This is Wendy, John, Alan. We're Ligeia."

Ligeia. That was something from Edgar Allan Poe. Trudy had read the poem, had even been to the coast to see the island he'd written about in "The Gold-Bug." She liked the band already.

Their sound made Trudy think of a funeral in a Gothic cathedral, or the spooky look of the Low Country at dusk, Spanish moss hanging like cobwebs, bats flitting around. Noel's voice was low and menacing. He stood at the center of the stage, his hands cupped around the mic. From time to time he pressed his palms to his temples as if he were trying to quell demon voices. Although he barely moved, his body was tensed. Trudy expected him to pounce into the crowd like a panther. She kept her eyes on him for the entire show.

Afterwards, she climbed over the side of the loft and descended the stairs. She found Noel lounging against the wall in the Pink Room, smoking a cigarette.

"Hey, why don't you move around a little more onstage?" she said. "You looked like an old man hunched over the microphone."

He reached up slowly and pushed his glasses down his nose far enough so that she could see the contempt in his eyes. "What's it to you, little girl?"

She wondered if she would see all that pent-up energy let loose then. But no. He looked at her for a long moment, repositioned his glasses, and flicked the ash of his cigarette on her. Then he turned on his heel and walked away.

Trudy had felt something crackle between them and she couldn't stop thinking about it. It was like a live wire, flailing around, spewing electricity into the universe. A force that could be guided and harnessed and used for something spectacular.

She had to have him.

Over the next week, she carried out her recon mission. There was nothing coy about her questions. It was clear to all she asked that she had designs on that thin, white body, those long bones.

"Forget it, Trudy," Johnny Fad advised. "He's living with the bass player. I think they're engaged."

The story about Wendy was that she was a witch. She was working some kind of juju on Noel. She belonged to a coven. Well, Trudy had some tricks of her own and she wasn't above making her own gris-gris.

She went home that first night, her shirt still smudged with ash, and wrote him a letter: "You don't know me, but we are like meteors hurling toward each other. Meet me tomorrow night on the fire escape of the Heart of Dixie Motel and I'll tell you your future." She didn't sign her name. Mystery would work in her favor.

He was there, as she knew he would be. It was dark, the night sky clouded, not even a moon. All she saw at first was a red ember as he sucked in smoke. As she moved up the iron stairs, she imagined she was in a movie, a camera following the sway of her hips, the way her hand trailed the iron railing. And then, face to face, she felt shy. There was a force field around him—she could feel it—and she had to push her way in.

He blew a stream of smoke into her face. "What do you want from me?"

And she said, "Everything."

It wasn't as if she wanted it for free. She was willing to barter. She reached into her pocket and took out a tape.

"Bootleg Joy Division. Taped live in Manchester. The only copy in the world." She waved it slowly under his nose. Her investigation had revealed that Noel worshipped the ghost of '70s legend Ian Curtis, the band's suicidal genius.

He seemed unimpressed. Took another drag. But then he reached out for the cassette and examined it in the borrowed light of a street lamp. "Is the sound quality any good?"

"You'll have to give it a listen and find out." Trudy knew from the way that his eyes, and then his feet, followed her down the clattery steps that he was at least intrigued.

Back in her room, they cleared away circles of carpet and propped themselves against the wall. Trudy jammed the tape into her boom box and they sat there, deep in the music.

"Wow. This is good stuff," Noel said after the first song. "It almost sounds professionally recorded. Where'd you get it?"

"From my dad. He's got a great music collection. There's more where this came from." Trudy could see the points stacking up in her favor. "So what are your parents like?"

Noel told her that he'd been disowned.

"Yeah, me too, more or less." Trudy said. So they had something in common. "What did you do you?"

"They caught me with a guy."

Uh, oh. "You mean . . . you're gay?"

"Naw. I prefer women." He gave her a long look, and once again she felt the air crackle. "It was just a one-time thing. I was curious, that's all. But my mom and dad thought I was the Antichrist after that."

Trudy sometimes wondered what it would be like with another girl. She'd once had a dream about kissing Cassie, of all people. In the dream, Cassie had been fleshy and voluptuous like Marilyn Monroe. In real life, her type would be someone thin. Like Noel.

"You have star quality," Trudy told him. "I feel it here." She pressed a hand against her belly.

Noel snorted. "What do you know about it?"

"My dad was in a band. He knows lots of famous musicians. They came over to our apartment and with some of them you could feel the air changing. It was like weather. I'm telling you, you have it."

He stared at the ceiling. Trudy couldn't tell if he was musing or spacing out. She decided to go on. "But I think you should get rid of Wendy. There's something creepy about her and she's so . . . retro."

He didn't answer at first, but then he rolled his head to look at her and raised an eyebrow.

"I can play the guitar," she said.

And she could, a little. Her father had given her a few lessons on his acoustic guitar, back when she was still living with him. She'd been practicing on her own, too. So far he hadn't noticed his guitar was missing. He called her every now and then, and he hadn't mentioned it yet. Jack was more into African rhythms these days. He had a set of drums handcrafted by a Yoruban tribesman.

"You'd probably destroy the stage," Noel said. He knew all about her.

Trudy laughed. "Flatter me some more."

"You're a walking disaster," he drawled. "You're the embodiment of sin."

"Trudy Sin," she said, trying it on for size. She was sick of all her other names, fed up with stepfathers and their counterfeit legacies. Sick of her father. Sick of Sarah.

"Speaking of sin," Trudy said. She scooted over to him and started to pull her shirt off.

He grabbed her by the shoulders. "Listen, Trudy. I like you. But I'm engaged to Wendy."

"Things can change," Trudy said.

12

"Hey, Gil?" Harumi dragged a wet cloth over the top of the bar. "Can I leave a couple of hours early tonight?"

Gil, the manager of Goatfeathers, turned away from the cappuccino maker and stroked one of his sideburns with a finger. "We'll see. If we're not too busy."

At the moment, only three tables were occupied. There was also one guy sitting at the big table in the center of the coffee bar, leafing through the glossy foreign magazines. Harumi knew him. Chip. Her favorite customer. He was just about the nicest and cutest guy she'd ever met. He was a stockbroker, a regular, and he tipped well. Even if he just had a bottle of Red Stripe, he'd leave two dollars. Harumi wasn't sure about the others. One table had ordered cheesecake. The others were just having coffee. So far this wasn't looking like a big money night.

Things could change, though. It was six P.M. on a Friday night. College kids would go out drinking at the bars around Five Points and come in to sober up with French Roast and espresso later on. Yuppie couples who'd managed to snag babysitters usually crowded in around ten. Places like Rockafellas and The Cave were too young and loud for the young professional types, but at Goatfeathers, where there was abstract art on the walls, Jamaican beer on the menu, and Josephine Baker on the stereo, they could feel artsy and sophisticated. The yuppies left good tips.

Harumi had been working there for two months now. She knew she hadn't been hired because of her extensive waitressing experience; she had none. This was her first job.

Gil hired staff for their looks. He liked dyed hair (obvious, but not outrageous; he wouldn't go for pink), men with pierced ears and makeup, and ethnicity. He was also concerned with clothes. There was no uniform at Goatfeathers, but Gil wouldn't employ someone who didn't have a cool wardrobe.

Harumi had shown up for her interview wearing a little black silk sheath and huge earrings of wavery copper that almost touched her shoulders. She'd bought them in a little art gallery down the street. For her meeting with Gil, she'd swept her hair into a fountain and made up her eyes with gold and purple eye shadow. She'd barely had to say a word. He hadn't even asked if she was of legal age.

Harumi had just turned eighteen. In less than a year, she'd be finished with high school. And then? She didn't know yet.

She'd sent for college application forms just to make her parents stop whimpering, but she hadn't filled them out yet. She needed time to figure out what she wanted to do. For the first time in her life, she could choose.

After she'd destroyed her violin, Harumi had spent months in therapy. Her parents believed that the music had made her crazy. They refused to consider the possibility that her outburst had had anything to do with them.

"The doctor said not to push you," Mrs. Yokoyama wailed. "But, Harumi, what is it you want to do?"

The day she'd presented Harumi with a new sheaf of college applications she'd said, "You don't have to be concert violinist. You can be music teacher. Not so much pressure."

Harumi hadn't touched a violin in almost a year. Sometimes she dreamed that she held Sadie. She dreamed of auditoriums crashing with applause, roses strewn across the stage, and she'd woken feeling sad.

Not anymore. These days she had Zelda—her red secondhand Rickenbacker, which she played every day. She practiced in the basement with an amp. When she emerged from the musty gloom, from the boxes of Christmas ornaments and the mousetraps and Koji's high chair, her mother always looked worried.

Harumi could tell by the lines on her forehead and the hound dog droop of her eyes that she hated the bass, that she didn't understand her daughter's strange compulsion, but that she couldn't say a word. Doctor's orders. So she kept her mouth shut until she could spill her thoughts to her lunch group.

Harumi had once overheard them as they sat in the Yokoyama kitchen with their egg salad sandwiches. They all thought that she was in her room doing homework, but she was spying from the hallway.

"It's not normal for a girl like that to play the guitar," her mother said.

"Maybe you could get her to take *koto* lessons," Mrs. Nakano replied. She had a fresh-off-the-boat accent. "She might enjoy something a bit more genteel."

"It'll pass. Don't worry." Harumi recognized Mrs. Kimura's voice. "She's just going through a phase. Our Yuki decided that she hated math when she was in junior high school and now she's going to major in physics."

"A phase? You really think so?" Mrs. Yokoyama sniffled as if she'd been crying.

"It could be worse," Mrs. Nakano said. "She could be pregnant or on drugs. These American kids are really wild, not like the ones back in Japan."

Of course she wasn't pregnant. She wasn't even allowed to date. Until recently, she hadn't been permitted to go out at night with friends. Ridiculous. Her parents didn't know about the band. If they found out about it, they'd probably put her in a straitjacket. On the nights when they had a gig, her parents thought she was sleeping over at Esther Shealy's house. Although they didn't approve of Esther, they didn't say anything. They were afraid to criticize or advise, afraid that she might break something else.

Esther Shealy. Harumi thought of her now as she cleared away Chip's empty beer bottle and pocketed the five-dollar bill he'd left for her. She'd known Esther almost all of her life, or at least she thought she had. After that scene at that party they'd gone to together she wasn't so sure. It's not that she disapproved. She knew that some people were gay and if Esther was attracted to women, she was probably born that way. But Harumi realized later, after the shock of seeing her kissing that woman, that Esther was a stranger. What else was she hiding?

At the same time, she was thinking about how little she knew about love and sex in general. She knew how to tune a violin, but she didn't know how to flirt. She was intimate with the music of Chopin, but she'd never kissed a boy—or girl, for that matter.

Everyone thought that she was so worldly because she'd been to New York and performed onstage with adults, but all those years with Sadie had robbed her of experience of another kind. She didn't know how to move in the world without an instrument.

Cassie came through the door in combat boots and an oversized black dress scribbled with Technicolor graffiti just as Harumi's shift was ending. She finished wiping the tables, punched her time card, and grabbed her bass and amp from the back room.

"My car's right outside," Cassie said. "We could walk, but it's dark."

Harumi followed her to the curb and they got in the car.

"Ready for the big audition?"

Harumi felt a flash of panic. Auditions had always made her feel like throwing up. But this would be different. Cassie had already told her all about Trudy, how she didn't know how to play any instruments herself, and how eager she'd been when Cassie had offered to introduce Harumi to her. She understood that there was no competition for the position, and that Trudy was borderline desperate for a drummer. All Harumi had to do was show up.

When they got to the house where Trudy lived, they saw her sitting on the porch, in a pool of light. She sprang up to meet them as soon as they got out of the car.

"Perfect timing," she said. "My roommate's still at work, so we can be as noisy as we want."

The neighboring houses were dark. Did that mean that everyone was sleeping? Harumi didn't want to wake anybody up.

"Hey," Trudy said to Harumi, suddenly a little shy. "I like your earrings."

Harumi reached up and touched the rhinestone Eiffel Towers dangling from her lobes. "Thanks."

Cassie had told her that appearances were important to Trudy, that she had a certain look in mind for Screaming Divas. It was a good sign that she liked her jewelry.

They moved inside to a dimly lit living room. The faint smell of cigarettes and burnt toast lingered in the air. The worn, stained carpet had vacuum tracks, as if Trudy had just finished sweeping.

"Can I get you a drink or something?" she asked, all puppy-like.

"No, thanks. I'm good." After carrying trays of beer and coffee beverages around all night, Harumi didn't want to look at a glass. She looked around for an outlet, somewhere to set up.

"So Cassie told me that you went to Juilliard," Trudy said. Her eyes were shiny.

"I, uh, tried out. I didn't go." Cassie must not have mentioned her breakdown, which was just as well.

"Oh."

"So do you want me to play something?"

"Sure." Trudy flopped down on the sofa. The coils whined beneath her. "If you want."

"I told her about your other band," Cassie put in.

Harumi cringed. She didn't want to think about those guys. She hoped that this new band would take themselves seriously. At the very least, she hoped they planned on practicing.

Cassie sat down on the sofa beside Trudy, as if she were settling in for a performance.

Harumi plugged in the amp, slowly unzipped the case, and brought out Zelda. When she was finally ready, she looked up at Trudy, who was leaning forward, waiting for some sign of genius. The fingers of Harumi's left hand began crawling over the frets like spiders, while she strummed out the first bars of "Für Elise" with her pick. At the sight of Trudy's puzzled expression, she bit back a smile, and then segued into "Bela Lugosi's Dead."

Trudy started humming along. Cassie's combat boot was tapping. Harumi stopped worrying about the neighbors and gave herself over to the bassline. By the time she got to the end of the song, no one was sitting down.

"So do you want to join up?" Trudy asked.

That was it? The audition was over? "Uh, sure."

Trudy reached out her hand as if they were a couple of businessmen. They shook.

"Well, alright then. I hereby declare you a Screaming Diva."

13

Esther was alone in the gallery, flicking a feather duster over the sculptures and furniture. She was in a meditative state, bathed in New Age harp music. Then the bell on the door tinkled and Rebecca appeared.

"Guess what? We're having a party!"

Esther put the feather duster under the counter. "A party?

"An art show. A gallery opening. You remember that bloke Adam? The one who made the coat of arms out of a garbage can lid? We're going to represent his work."

"Cool." Esther pictured herself flitting from guest to guest with a plate of canapés.

"And I have the most brilliant idea," Rebecca went on. "Why don't we ask your friend—the little Japanese girl—and her band to play? It would be purr-fect. Trash art, trash music."

Esther felt as if her skin had suddenly become a size too small. She hadn't spoken to Harumi since that night in the car, since the night she'd met Rebecca. She knew that Harumi worked at that bohemian coffee shop on the next block, but there was no point in going there. Their friendship had crashed and burned.

"Well, uh, actually that band broke up," Esther said, not meeting Rebecca's eyes. "She's in a new band now. A girl band."

"How fabulous. Even better."

Esther shifted her weight, trying to think of some sort of response. She wondered what Rebecca would make of Cassie. Maybe she'd go after her with the same kind of intensity she'd used in seducing Esther—the prowl and then the pounce. For a few seconds, Esther imagined the two of them clawing at each other, but it was Rebecca she was jealous of, not Cassie. She closed her eyes and choked back her fear.

"What's the band's name?"

"Uh, Screaming Divas. I think."

"Fabulous! I love it!"

"They haven't actually performed in public yet. I don't know if they're any good."

"Darling, they don't have to be good. We want something rough to go with the feel of Adam's work. Think of it as performance art, not music."

She crossed the gallery and reached out to stroke Esther's cheek. "Please, darling, will you ask your friend? As a favor to me?"

Later, after a woman had bought a string of hand-painted clay beads, after a pair of Yankee tourists had waltzed off with a signed Blue Sky print, Esther said goodbye for the day and rounded the corner to Goatfeathers.

She'd been there a few times before on coffee breaks with Rebecca, but never during Harumi's shift.

The interior was dark. Most of the tables were empty, though Esther spotted a thirtysomething guy in a blue Oxford shirt at the center table. He was leafing through a dog-eared copy of *Architectural Digest*. A group of students in USC regalia and crew cuts were crammed into one booth. Empty beer bottles cluttered their table.

As Esther walked by, she heard one guy say, "Hey, get Connie Chung over here. We need more brewski." The others laughed.

Esther felt that old anger rise within her. Her first impulse was to grab one of those empty beer bottles and bring it down on the guy's prickly head. He was big, though—meaty and stupid—and she knew she'd lose the fight. She might end up with a broken head herself. But she couldn't just ignore the remark.

She turned to the booth and said, "For your information, your waitress is named Harumi. And her roots are Japanese, not Chinese."

They stared at her for a moment. Then the ringleader smiled and said, "Who the hell are you?"

Esther could feel someone coming up behind her. She moved out of the way and Harumi brushed by.

"Hey, guys. More beer?"

Esther watched for a moment as Harumi loaded a tray with clinking bottles, and then climbed on a stool across from Blue Oxford Shirt. He looked up and smiled at her.

Harumi was beautiful and confident, Esther thought. She didn't need anyone to defend her from the bigots and assholes of the world. Look at the way she held herself—back straight, chin high, eyes cool. She held everything important deep inside and there was no getting at it.

Esther watched her one-time best friend come toward her, pad in hand.

"Hey, Esther. What'll it be?"

Esther's heart was ticking like a bomb. All of the words she wanted to say jammed in her throat.

Harumi waited, her face blank. "Here's a menu. I'll give you a few minutes." She went back to Blue Oxford. "Another Red Stripe, Chip?"

It was hard to believe they'd once chased the ice cream truck together and traded Nancy Drew books. To Harumi, Esther was just another customer, another tip that she had to hustle for.

When she returned, Esther still hadn't opened the menu, but she knew what she wanted. "I'll have a café au lait," she said. "But I came here to ask you a favor."

14

"A gig!" Trudy whooped and jumped around the room. "We've got a gig!" What's more, it would be at Adam's opening. She would show him that she wasn't just some little girl. She was a *contender*.

"You mean you'll do it?" the little Earth Mama said.

Trudy didn't know anything about Esther, but she liked her already. This neo-hippie in layered gauze and wooden beads was the angel of rock-and-roll bookings. She would have a special place in punk rock heaven. Trudy would remember what she had done for them when the biographers and interviewers appeared with their pads of paper, eager to know every detail of Screaming Divas' history. Or herstory.

Harumi scowled from across the room. She stroked her bass as if it were some kind of talisman. Trudy noticed that she always did this when she was tense about something. "We need to practice," she said. "A lot. And Cassie needs to learn how to play that guitar."

"Well, don't practice too much," the tall blonde woman named Rebecca said. "We'd like the music to be, y'know, rough."

Trudy nodded. Rebecca didn't look rough at all. She, in her tight black suit and herringbone stockings, made all of the furniture in Trudy's living room look especially shoddy. But this woman was in tune like no other. She understood, as Harumi didn't, that they would be playing for the people, not a bunch of society bores in tuxes and mink. She knew that their appeal rose above their inability to sustain a beat.

"We don't have a drummer," Cassie said.

"We'll find one," Trudy said quickly. "Esther? Do you want to be our drummer?"

Esther's pale face turned red. "Me? I, uh, I have no musical experience."

"Just kidding," Trudy said. "Seriously. I have someone in mind."

"At ease, girls. I'm sure you'll be fabulous."

"Well, let's break out the booze and celebrate!" Without waiting for a response, Trudy marched into the kitchen, reached into the fridge, and filled her arms with Corona. She wished that they had champagne, but anything that fizzed a little would do. Back in the living room, she passed out the drinks.

"One for you," she said, handing a bottle to Rebecca. "And one for you," to Harumi. When she held out a beer to Cassie, she shook her head, as usual.

"No, thanks."

Trudy was disappointed for a split second. She thought that just this once, on this most auspicious occasion of landing their first gig ever, Cassie might imbibe. But no. And Trudy understood. She knew about her mother's drinking problem and about the accident that had wrecked Cassie's face.

They popped open the beers and toasted their impending success. Trudy sat cross-legged on the middle of the floor at Rebecca's feet.

This woman was way cool. And she could help Screaming Divas conquer Columbia. "Can you drum, Rebecca?" Trudy asked.

"Probably." Rebecca took a long draught and winked at Esther, who was sitting silently in the corner.

Esther, Trudy noted, suddenly looked very uncomfortable. She sat, back straight, knees together, as if she were at a job interview or something. What was her deal? Harumi had mentioned that Esther was an old friend and Cassie knew her from school. Trudy sensed that there were secrets to be uncovered. Well, there was time enough for that.

"Who's going to sing?" Harumi asked now. She'd put down her bass, but her mind was still on technicalities.

During practice, Trudy and Cassie took turns as lead diva. Cassie sang the songs she'd written and thrashed around the room; Trudy did her Screaming Divas versions of Supremes songs. But alone, when the others had packed up and gone home, Trudy practiced Cassie's songs. She copied Cassie's movements in front of the mirror and worked menace into her voice. She knew that she could do the songs as well as Cassie.

Here in the living room, Trudy and Cassie exchanged glances. Trudy stared hard, willing Cassie to give in.

"It's your band," she said, dropping her gaze. "You can sing. I think I'd be more comfortable in the background anyhow."

"We'll all be singing," Trudy said. "We'll all be screaming and dancing and having a ball."

15

Well, why couldn't she be a drummer? Esther tapped her chopsticks against her bowl. What was so funny about the idea of her drumming? If she practiced, she was sure that she could do it.

"A dollar for your thoughts, luv," Rebecca said from the other side of the table.

This was Esther's birthday dinner. She wouldn't turn eighteen till the following day, but she'd be going out to some family restaurant with her parents and they'd be eating cake and ice cream together. She couldn't invite Rebecca to join them. It would be too weird.

On her last birthday, Harumi had slept over and they'd watched old movies. Harumi had given her a bracelet. This year, she'd be lucky if she got a card from her.

Of course Rebecca had given her a gift. Earlier, in Rebecca's apartment, Esther had been handed a shoebox, wrapped in silver paper and decorated with tendrils of blue ribbon. She'd felt a gush of excitement as she shook the box and felt something rattling around inside.

"Come on, darling. Open it." Rebecca was leaning forward and Esther could tell that she was eager to tug at the ribbons herself.

In spite of Rebecca's impatience, she did her best to prolong the moment. She removed the ribbons and coiled them beside her, then slit the tape with her fingernail.

Rebecca's manicured nails drummed on the arm of her chair.

Finally, Esther lifted the lid, parted the tissue paper, and stared into the box. She'd never seen anything like it, so at first she wasn't sure what it was. It was long and white and plastic and there was a little switch. A curling iron? Esther took the thing out of the box and flicked the switch. It began to hum and vibrate in her hand. She tentatively touched it to the back of her neck, where the nerves were tight. Maybe this thing was supposed to reduce stress or something.

Rebecca was watching her with a mischievous smile.

"Umm, what is it?" Esther finally asked.

"It's an orgasm machine," Rebecca whispered. "I couldn't think of anything I'd rather give you more."

Esther blushed. She couldn't imagine a more embarrassing gift. This was worse than the training bra her grandmother had once given her for Christmas and that she'd unwittingly unwrapped in front of the entire family. And what was she going to do with it? If her mother found it, she'd freak. "Well, thanks," Esther said.

Rebecca smiled. "It's my pleasure, entirely. Now I don't know about you, luv, but I'm famished. Is Chinese okay?"

So here they were, with their rice and jasmine tea, listening to plucked strings in the Jade Pagoda Restaurant.

"I was thinking about that band. The one we booked for the art show."

Rebecca nodded, encouraging her.

"I was thinking that it would be cool to be in a band. To be the drummer, maybe." That was kind of a lie. Esther knew that her interest in Screaming Divas had more to do with Cassie. If she were in the band, she could see Cassie almost every day. She could stare at her golden hair from behind her drum kit and breathe in her perfume.

And Harumi. Maybe they'd be able to patch up their friendship. They'd finally have something in common. Esther missed Harumi, and seeing her at Goatfeathers and in Trudy's living room made the feeling sharper. Sure, she had Rebecca, but these days there was no one in her life her own age, no one who knew her background.

16

Trudy kept watch from her crow's nest. She set the needle in the groove, cued up the next record, and leaned over the railing to scan the crowd. If she craned her neck, she could see the top of the narrow, graffiti-lined staircase, and Jan checking IDs at the door. Inside the club, people leaned against the brick walls or balanced on wooden stools, the tips of their cigarettes flaring like fireflies.

Noel hadn't been to The Cave in three weeks. Trudy imagined his home life: Wendy screaming, "A hex on you if you walk out that door!" When he finally showed up, alone, no less, she thought she was seeing things.

"Shit." Trudy glanced at the spinning vinyl and shrugged. "Let them listen to all of side one." She hurdled over the railing and climbed down the ladder.

Trudy homed in on Noel immediately. "Hey, stranger. Where've you been?"

"Trudy." He wobbled a bit as he slung an arm over her shoulder. He'd obviously had a few. Was this a sign of trouble in paradise?

She tossed her hair back. "I've got a band now."

"So I've heard."

He was keeping track of her—another good sign.

"Truth is," Trudy said, leaning in close enough to taste the beer on his breath, "we've got a gig coming up, but we don't have a drummer."

"And?" Noel's mouth was inches from hers.

"And I was wondering if we might borrow Alan."

"I'll talk to him," Noel said.

Trudy could feel his hand gliding over her hips. He'd never touched her like this in public before. Either he was out-of-control drunk, or things were so bad with Wendy that he didn't care what kind of rumors got back to her.

"Do you want to come over later?" Trudy asked.

"I'm almost a married man."

"You say it like you mean it," she said, teasing. She could tell just by looking at him that he was hot for her. Anyway, who got married at nineteen? She ran her thumbnail over his fly, then whirled away. "I've got to change the record. These people aren't dancing."

Five minutes later, Noel was gone.

Trudy asked Johnny Fad to take over in the DJ booth and went in search of him. He wasn't standing in line for the bathroom or leaning against the wall smoking a cigarette. He wasn't in the Pink Room either, but Cassie and Harumi were, sipping Diet Cokes and watching the pool game through gauzy smoke.

"Have you seen Noel?" she asked.

Harumi shook her head.

"No," Cassie said. "I didn't even know he was here."

Trudy was about to bolt off, to check the sidewalk and the area surrounding the building, but Cassie grabbed her arm.

"Just chill with us for a moment, okay?" she said.

Trudy was still tense, ready to pounce on Noel the minute she saw him. "I think he's getting ready to leave Wendy," she said. "He was kneading my ass in front of everyone."

Harumi listened politely, her face blank, but Cassie rolled her eyes.

"You deserve much better. Why settle for Noel when you could have someone who really cares about you? You ought to hold out for someone who's crazy about you, who'd be willing to cut his wrists if you asked him to."

"Have you ever been in love before, Cassie?"

She shrugged. "Sure."

Trudy figured that was a lie. If she'd experienced real love, she'd know that it was like a freight train bearing down on you and there was nothing you could do to stop it. Even if the guy was an ax murderer, it's not as if you could control how you felt about him.

"*Women Who Love Too Much*—ever hear of that book?" Cassie asked, digging her in the ribs. "I think Johnette's got a copy. I could borrow it for you."

"Ha ha." Trudy knew where she was coming from. She'd heard about Cassie's mother, how the woman had been a doormat for her husband. It was easy to understand that Cassie wouldn't want to be like that, crying herself to sleep every night, escaping in booze. But love, that was the thing that made living worthwhile.

"So, Cassie, if you could have anyone here, who would you choose?"

Cassie looked slowly around the room. One of the guys playing pool was pretty hot. He was tall and slender with a pulpy mouth and deep-set eyes. And then there was Jeff, the David Bowie lookalike, dressed in black as usual, a tuft of bright blond hair peeking out from under his caballero hat, enigmatic as ever.

Finally, Cassie turned back to Trudy and smirked. "I guess I'd choose you," she said. "You, or Harumi."

At the sound of her name, Harumi looked up, startled, then back down into her Coke.

"How about you, Harumi?" Trudy needled.

She was silent for a moment, then said, "I think Johnny Fad is divine. I'd take that boy over Noel any day."

They all laughed, realizing the sheer impossibility of the match-up.

"Yeah, well, we have each other. That's all that matters, right?" Trudy was suddenly intoxicated by sisterhood. She'd never had friends before, not really.

They could hear the start of a song, and the bouncy beat lured them to the dance floor.

"Hey, we can do it better than those girls," Trudy said, nodding toward the speakers. "I'm going to beg Jan to give us a gig."

17

"Junk art" was right, Cassie thought when she walked into the gallery. The place looked like a garage sale after a tornado had been through it. Pedestals around the room were laden with twisted and welded bits of metal. Coat hangers, hubcaps, mangled rubber baby dolls, dirty tennis shoes, broken plates. At first glance, nothing made sense. She stooped to read some of the labels: "All God's Children Can Dance." "End of the Millennium." "The Crying of Lot 49." Nothing made sense at second glance either.

Oh, well. At least they didn't have to worry about people slamming and breaking stuff. And it would be pretty damn intimidating to play in a room full of Picassos or even at a Blue Sky exhibit. Besides, what did she know about modern art? Maybe this guy was a genius.

The bits and pieces of crashed cars all around her made her think of the accident. Inevitably, she thought of her mother.

Mama had loved her more than the moon and stars, more than her daddy, more than the whiskey that swirled over the ice in her cut-crystal goblet each night, more than God, even. And Mama had loved to dress her up in miniature evening gowns and Little Bo Peep outfits and two-piece bathing suits with frilly panties. Loved to brush her long buttery locks till Cassie's scalp started to get sore, loved to decorate her face with the perfumed creams and powders she bought at Tapp's cosmetics counter. Cassie had been her honey baby, her sweetie princess.

She would have been proud on a night like this one, to see Cassie taking the stage again. Maybe she was sitting on a cloud up in heaven with her glass of whiskey, ice cubes tinkling as she looked down on the scene.

Cassie wrapped her arms around her torso. She had to get her mind on other things. Already a headache was hatching at the base of her skull. She wouldn't be able to sing if her head was banging with pain.

"Hey, Cassie."

She turned and saw Esther Shealy. "Wow. You look different."

Esther's hair had been harnessed and styled into a modest beehive. She'd poured herself into a strapless gown.

"You look ravishing," Esther said. "But you always look great."

Cassie had a vague sense of déjà vu, but it floated away before she could grab on and analyze it. "Thanks. Where's Rebecca?"

Cassie wasn't sure, but she thought there was something going on between Esther and Rebecca. Maybe they were lovers.

Cassie wondered what that might be like—doing it with a woman. Sometimes, when she was too tired to drive back home after band practice, she spent the night in Trudy's bed. They'd talk for a while and cuddle like sisters, and then drift into sleep with their legs entwined. When Trudy was asleep, she'd sometimes throw her arm over Cassie's body. Once, her palm had landed on Cassie's breast. She hadn't pushed it away. She'd reached over and cupped Trudy's breast, and rubbed her nipple with her thumb until Trudy moaned and stirred. In the morning, neither of them said anything about touching each other.

Rebecca appeared then, a goddess in an orange vinyl sheath.

A tall, gangly young man with black hair and a length of chain through his belt loops tiptoed up behind her. He growled and sank his teeth into Rebecca's pale neck.

"Adam, darling, I was wondering where you'd gotten off to." Rebecca reached up and patted him on the head. Then she turned and kissed him on the lips.

Cassie checked Esther's face, saw that she was ill at ease. She tried to think of something to say, but Rebecca sent her on an errand and she found herself standing alone with Adam.

"So you're Trudy's friend, huh?"

"Yeah, so?"

Of course she knew about Adam and Trudy. Before Noel had entered the picture, Trudy had talked about Adam constantly—how he'd been her first love, how her dad had caught them in bed, how she'd been his muse. She'd heard about the fire from someone else.

"Did she give you that scar?" he asked her.

Cassie's hand flew automatically to her face. Most people made an effort to keep their eyes on the pretty half. They were far too polite to ever bring up the ridge of tissue. She'd been thinking that she'd go in for cosmetic surgery soon, but Trudy had convinced her to leave it alone. She'd even forgone her usual makeup job, not expecting that her scar would immediately become a topic of conversation.

Adam was watching her, waiting for her to answer.

"I was in an accident." Cassie gestured at the sculptures, the detritus of other collisions. "It happened when I was little." She tried to blow it off, to make it seem like something almost forgotten, but the night played over and over in her mind.

She was curled under bedcovers, trying to block out the fight downstairs and then her mother came into the room and a shaft of light fell across the bed.

"Come on, sweetie. We're going for a drive . . . ."

Adam was staring at her.

"What?"

"I don't know. Your face. It's so interesting. I'd like to paint it."

Cassie laughed.

"No, really. Would you sit for me? A couple of hours?"

He reached over and touched her jaw lightly. Attraction sizzled through her.

Cassie didn't believe that he knew how to paint. This room was filled with the junk heaps of a grease monkey. Maybe he was feeding her a line, but she liked it.

She thought she might like Adam, too. He was different from the boys she'd gone out with till now. He wouldn't think that dropping in on The Cave would make a freak out of her. He'd been with Trudy, after all.

Trudy. Cassie wondered how she'd react if she went out with Adam. Lately, Trudy's obsession with him seemed to have died down, but maybe she was just pretending to be over him. Behind that tough exterior, Trudy was raw, vulnerable. She needed love and attention, and lots of it. Wasn't that part of what being in this band was all about? Well, Cassie could keep a secret. She wanted Adam. She was pretty sure he wanted her. Trudy wouldn't ever have to know.

As if she had been summoned, Trudy herself burst through the door. Cassie watched the swivel of her neck as she checked out every nook and cranny, obviously searching for Noel. All she had talked about for three days was Noel and whether or not he would show up for their debut. She said that she was sure he'd be there, lured by her insistent charm, but Cassie knew beneath her bravado, she had her doubts.

Trudy's gaze finally came to a rest on Cassie and Adam, and she made a beeline for them.

"Cassie!" She looped her arm around her waist and smacked her on the cheek, then nodded coolly at Adam.

"Trudy," Adam said, stepping away.

Cassie watched Adam for a moment, admiring his feline movement, until another stab of pain distracted her.

If anyone could provide her with immediate medication, it was the lead diva. Trudy was a walking pharmacy with a pill for every mood. Cassie whispered her symptoms.

Trudy's face took on a glow. "I have just the thing." She rummaged around in her mudcloth bag (a souvenir from one of her dad's trips to Africa) and brought forth a handful of red capsules. "Take two and call me in an hour," Trudy said.

Cassie swallowed the pills without water and waited for them to take effect.

Harumi showed up then, on the heels of Alan, and they started setting up their equipment.

By the time the art lovers and scenesters started flowing through the door, Cassie's headache had been subdued. The pain had given way to a dreamy haze. Words felt heavy in her mouth. The air resisted her limbs. Still, she managed to drag herself onto the makeshift stage. She tuned her guitar and when Trudy gave the signal, her hands moved automatically.

They bullied their way through "I Hear a Symphony" and "Come See About Me" and "Baby Love."

Cassie looked out into the crowd and saw the heads bobbing, the feet tapping, people careful not to spill their drinks. Jan and Lynn, the owners of The Cave, danced at front and center. Incredibly, they seemed to be enjoying the music. It could be that they were just drunk, but maybe they really would let the Divas play at their club.

She saw Adam at the back, staring at her. Some woman with a pad of paper stood at his elbow. From time to time she scribbled something. A reporter, Cassie thought. And there was Noel, the infamous Noel, a wry smile pasted on his face. He probably thought their music was awful.

Cassie didn't care about the critics. She didn't even really care what the audience thought. She was riding on a magic carpet over fields of daisies. She felt lovely and lazy and warm.

At the front of the stage, Trudy was gasping, working up energy for the next number. She edged over toward Cassie and said, "Let's do 'Crashbaby.'"

Cassie nodded.

"Do you want to sing?"

Cassie shook her head. She didn't want anything to disturb the woozy, comfortable state she was in.

Trudy nodded, then tossed her head like a wet dog. Drops of sweat splattered the stage.

How weird to watch Trudy thrash around singing her song. Cassie's lips moved with the words that she had scrawled on paper. Those words had risen from her memories, from the core of her, from a black night long ago. Now, they were floating over the heads of the young men and women in their little black dresses and thrift shop jackets. They were weaving among the junk sculptures, sailing out the window and to the moon.

The rest of the evening passed like a dream. During "Lady Lazarus Rises Again," someone accidentally knocked one of Adam's pieces onto the floor and the music was stopped. Adam raged around like a Picasso bull, calling Trudy names.

Cassie was too whacked out to drive home, so she crashed on Trudy's sofa. She didn't crawl into bed with her as usual, because Noel went home with them, too.

Cassie remembered thinking that it was odd because Noel was living with Wendy, but then again, her father had slept with other women when he'd been married to her mother. Men were like that. She heard Trudy giggling on the other side of her door, and then she dove into a deep sleep.

She woke once to the smell of cigarette smoke and Noel sitting in the corner, staring at her. In the morning, she wasn't sure whether he'd really been there or not.

18

When Harumi stumbled into the kitchen for breakfast, she was surprised to see her father there. Normally on a Saturday morning he would rise with the robins, eat quickly, and start in on the chores of the day. He'd have the lawn mower cranked before most decent people were out of bed. And on the days that he allowed himself leisure, he'd be the first one out on the golf course, the first fisherman on the lake. So what was he doing, still reading the newspaper at half past nine?

"What is this?" he asked as soon as she walked into the room.

Harumi plopped down on her chair and reached for the carton of orange juice. Her ears were still ringing from the night before and cigarette smoke clung to her hair.

Mr. Yokoyama stabbed his finger at the newspaper, at a black and white photo buried somewhere between world news and sports. "I said, what is this?"

Harumi wasn't a morning person. She liked to eat her corn flakes in silence as she gathered her thoughts around her. Usually the only other person at the table was Koji, and he was too busy wolfing down toast and eggs to think of conversation. It was too early in the morning for the harangue she felt coming on.

Harumi reached for the newspaper then, when her father refused to hand it over, got out of her chair to look over his shoulder.

The newspaper was opened to the arts page, something that rarely interested her father. She read the headline: "A Gallery of Garbage Draws More Than Flies." She looked at the pictures. There was a photo of one of Adam's sculptures, a figure of a man made out of bicycle handlebars, paint cans, wire, and hubcaps all welded together. Next to that was a picture of the band: Trudy sneering into the camera, Cassie bent over her guitar in fierce concentration, Harumi contorted with her bass in the air. Alan was lost in the grainy shadows, which was just as well since he wasn't a real band member. Their names were printed underneath.

"Oh, no," she whispered under her breath.

Then she felt the sting of a slap. She pressed her palm to her face. For a moment, she could only stare at this slump-shouldered man, her father. He had never struck her before. She could tell by the way that he lowered his eyes that he was ashamed of his actions, but she knew that he would never apologize.

"What was that for?" she asked. She wouldn't shout or cry. She would stay calm.

"You lied to us."

Yes, she had, but she was sure that there was more to his anger than that.

She could sense his struggle to find words to match his feelings. Her father rarely became angry. Mrs. Yokoyama was the one who ran around shrieking about every injustice that befell her. Mr. Yokoyama lacked the vocabulary for confrontations. He knew how to make rules, but he didn't know what to do when they were broken.

"And what is this name, 'Screaming Divas'? It sounds like a bunch of crazy women."

"It's just a name," Harumi said. "It doesn't mean anything."

"The newspaper says that you could not play your instruments well and that your music was junk. Like the sculptures."

Harumi felt as if she had been slapped again. No one had ever criticized her playing before. Besides, they hadn't been all that bad. Sure, Trudy's singing was off-key from song to song and Cassie's fingers fumbled once in a while, but they had energy. The crowd had enjoyed them. And she'd had a blast, up there on the stage with the Divas.

"Is that what you're mad about?" Harumi asked. "That some reporter says we played badly?"

She went back to her chair, weary from the fight. She grabbed a banana, although she'd suddenly lost her appetite, and began to peel it.

"No," her father said.

When Harumi looked up, she was shocked to see tears glistening in his eyes.

"I'm angry because you are wasting your talent. You were born to be a wonderful musician, and you betray yourself."

That old argument. Harumi felt doors clanging shut within herself. Why couldn't they just let her live her life? Let her have friends, a hobby, *a little fun once in a while*? For once in her life, she felt free and full of possibility, which was maybe odd since her musical potential was all that her family had focused on for as long as she could remember. But now she was making her own decisions, her own mistakes, and she was happy. Finally. Why couldn't they get lives of their own?

"No more rock 'n' roll," Mr. Yokoyama said, folding the newspaper. "I will buy you a new violin, if that's what you want."

Harumi watched him get up from the table and leave the room. She tore the banana peel into thinner and thinner strips.

There was no way she'd desert her friends. And no one was going to bash them in print like that ever again. They'd practice. Screaming Divas would become a legend.

19

Mrs. Shealy was hosing the flowerbed when Esther pulled into the driveway on Saturday afternoon. She watched her daughter park and climb out of her car with a load of metal.

"What in the world?"

"I'm going to be a drummer, Ma," Esther said.

Her mother bent down and turned off the water. "Are you out of your mind? You'll be going to college in the fall and you're working at the gallery. What do drums have to do with all this?"

"I'm going to be in a band," Esther said. "With Harumi."

Her mother rolled her eyes.

Okay, they both knew that, musically speaking, Harumi and Esther were worlds apart. When Harumi had been rising up through the ranks of the Suzuki School, Esther had begged her parents to let her learn to play the violin. Finally, after weeks of tears and tantrums, they'd given in. They couldn't afford Suzuki, but some cousin had an old violin in the attic that just needed dusting off, and a lady at the Baptist church gave lessons from her home.

Esther had tried hard, at first, to follow her instructor's directions. But daily practice was boring, and her mother, who was against the idea from the beginning, made no effort to discipline her. Running through the sprinkler and cutting paper dolls out of magazines was better for a child than trying to turn her into a mini-adult like Harumi.

After two months, Esther still couldn't read music and her bow's screech across the strings made the music teacher's dog howl with pain. "You're just wasting my time," the teacher said with a sigh. "You may as well go play."

Esther had cried all the way home. To make her feel better, her mother had dug up a pair of combs and a roll of wax paper. They'd made their own instruments and played music on the front porch. The violin was sent back to the cousin.

Well, drumming was about rhythm. Esther wasn't musically inclined, but she figured she could keep a beat.

Opportunity was arising. Esther had heard, one late night at The Cave after dancing for hours with Rebecca, that Alan might be leaving the band. Word had it that Noel was through playing house and ready to start up again. Ligeia was being brought back to life.

She'd found this drum kit at the Salvation Army store. It was dented and tarnished, but it would serve well for practice. If she could manage to sell that new Blue Sky assemblage that had come into the gallery last week, she could use the commission to invest in something better.

She struggled to get all the components out of her tiny hatchback.

Her mother didn't offer to help. She shook her head and went into the house.

A few hours later, they were all sitting around the dinner table—Esther's parents, Mark, and Esther. She wondered if they were the only family in America that ate together every night.

Esther's dad was still wearing his South Carolina Electric and Gas uniform. He spent all day scaling posts, fixing wires. The sun had burned deep lines in his face.

"So what's new?" he asked, as he did every night.

"Nothing," Mark mumbled, as usual, digging into a mound of mashed potatoes.

Esther didn't say anything. She'd tried to talk to her parents about the gallery, but they'd never heard of Blue Sky, they'd never even been to an art museum. They had absolutely no interest in art or her job.

"Esther's going to play drums in a band," her mother piped up.

"Drums?" Her father looked at her in disbelief. "Drumming is a man's job, isn't it? I've never heard of a girl playing the drums."

Esther sighed. Why did her parents have to be the dullest, least hip people on earth? "Get out of the Dark Ages, Dad. Women can do anything, haven't you heard? There are women doctors now. Women astronauts, women pumping gasoline."

Her father shrugged. "If you're trying to get a boyfriend, that might not be the right way to go about it. Guys might be afraid you'd start beating them with those sticks."

"Who says I'm trying to get a boyfriend?"

Esther knew that her parents worried about her. They'd married young, just out of high school. They didn't seem to understand Esther's apparent lack of a social life.

"Esther couldn't get a boyfriend even if she tried," Mark said with a chuckle.

"Shut up, wiener." Sometimes she wondered if he'd heard any rumors.

Someone's older brother or sister might have spotted her with Rebecca. And Rebecca herself was so indiscreet.

What would they do if they found out?

20

JAILBAIT
by Trudy Sin

I lied about my age
So you put Barbie in a cage.
Now I bleed into this song
so that you can sing along
with this girl upon the stage.

You thought that I was older.
I thought you would be bolder
and fight to keep me yours
but you bolted out the door.

(chorus)
Jailbait! Jailbait!
You knew that I was young.
Jailbait! Jailbait!
Yet your kiss was full of tongue.

You thought it was okay
till my dad walked in that day
and found us in his bed
and now he wants your head
and says I can't come out to play.

(chorus)

Late one afternoon at Goatfeathers, Trudy handed over a sheet of notebook paper full of smudges and scribbles to Cassie. "What do you think?"

Cassie studied the lyrics for a moment, twining a lock of hair in her finger as she read. She bit her lip.

"What?" Ugh. Trudy was sure she didn't like the song. She was probably trying to think of a nice way to say that it was crap.

"'Jailbait?'" Cassie asked, finally looking up.

"Yeah," Trudy confirmed. "That's the title."

"*Barbie in a cage / girl up on the stage.* This is about you and Adam, right?"

Trudy shrugged. "Yeah, so?"

Cassie lowered the paper, careful to avoid the cake crumbs and condensation puddles. She reached for Trudy's hand. "Do you still have feelings for him? Tell me the truth."

Well, she would always feel *something*. After all, he was the first. Her first lover, her first love, her first major heartbreak. How could she not feel anything? But she didn't want the Divas to think that she was a sap.

"Of course not," she said, steeling her spine. "But it's material, right? Got to find inspiration somewhere."

Cassie nodded slowly. "I like these lyrics. I think it could be a good song. Maybe Harumi would have ideas about the melody."

Trudy already had a track running in her head. She started humming, tapping out the beat on her knee. "The chorus, I was thinking, would be chanted. And y'all would yell out the 'jailbait' part."

Cassie stared at her for a moment. Then she said, "If you're really over Adam, then would you mind if I got with him?"

The song in her head went silent. Cassie and Adam? She'd seen them talking together at the gallery. At the time, she hadn't thought much of it. They seemed totally wrong for each other. But by the guilty look on her face, Trudy could tell that something had already happened between them. Well, she had Noel now. Or she would soon. Why not let Cassie and Adam be together?

"It's a free country," Trudy said finally. "Go ahead."

"Thanks." Cassie leaned back in the booth.

Trudy took a deep breath. She forced a smile, but it felt as if a boulder had suddenly landed in her stomach. She would never be completely over Adam. And she would never be over Noel.

21

Adam lived in a house in the Olympia section of Columbia, down by the prison, just this side of the fairgrounds. The houses in that area were falling apart and low rent, mostly inhabited by welfare recipients and college students. Nobody seemed to mow their lawn down there. It was Weed City. Cassie had heard rumors of drug deals and shootings. Her father had warned her not to venture beyond Blossom Street at night.

"A pretty girl like you," he said. "You never know what might happen."

People thought that good looks were dangerous. She remembered spying on her aunts one Christmas. The kids, Cassie included, were supposed to be playing Monopoly or pushing brand-new Tonka trucks through the shag carpeting. The men—the uncles and Cassie's father—were sprawled over the sofa, napping in front of college football on TV. The aunts, of course, were in the kitchen picking at cold turkey and homemade fudge, diets all gone to hell. They were caught up in their gossip and Cassie was sitting in the hallway, listening. Nobody knew she was there.

"She always envied that little girl." That was her daddy's oldest sister, Clara. The one with the big, ugly mole on her upper lip.

The other aunts, Belle and Dolores, clucked in agreement.

"Y'know, I'll bet she was trying to kill them both." It was still Clara talking. Clara always talked the most and had the most outrageous opinions.

"Aw, Clare. You don't think she meant to crash that car?"

Cassie could picture Aunt Clara's sloped shoulders rising and falling, her eyebrows arching. "You tell me. She was crazy jealous of her little beauty queen. There's no telling what was going on in her head."

At the time, Cassie had been too young to understand what the aunts were talking about. They might have been discussing some drugstore paperback. They never said her name, or her mother's, but the conversation had burrowed into her memory like chiggers into bare feet. It resurfaced in dreams, and sometimes when she was awake, like now, as she was driving to Adam.

Don't think about it, she told herself. Think about the future.

In less than a year, she'd be off to college and things would be great. She wouldn't have to listen to Johnette whining to her daddy about the gas man staring at her tits when he came to check the meter, or wheedling for money to buy a chunk of gaudy jewelry. She wouldn't have to listen to Jane Fonda panting on exercise videos. She'd be living in a dorm, going home only when she felt like it. Her life would be full of poetry and art and music. She'd have a passionate affair.

She found Adam's house without any trouble—one story, yellow paint, a hundred yards from the railroad tracks. (How did he get any sleep?) The front lawn was an expanse of dried, brown grass. Cassie parked her Bug on the edge of it, and hopped out of the car.

She could see herself reflected in the rolled-up window—sunlight bouncing off her golden hair, bare shoulders glistening with sweat, sunglasses giving her a Jackie O mystique.

A door opened and Adam stepped onto his cinderblock porch. He looked sickly pale in the afternoon sun. The long-sleeved black T-shirt and jeans didn't help.

"You made it," he said, his voice slow and heavy.

She wondered if he'd just woken up. He'd never told her how he earned a living. There was no way he made enough money from his art to pay rent and buy groceries.

The grass crunched beneath her feet. She followed him into the house and jumped when a ball of fur shot past.

"That's Mimi," he said. "One of my cats."

The carpet was matted with cat hair. This place rivaled Trudy's in filth. Cassie wrinkled her nose, but Adam didn't seem to notice.

"Welcome to my studio," he said, ushering her into a room at the back of the house. The hardwood floor was covered with paint-splattered newspapers. Some finished canvases were framed and stacked in a corner, facing the wall. A velveteen-upholstered chair stood at the center of the room.

"Sit there," Adam said. Then, remembering his manners, "Please."

Until this moment, Cassie had pictured a sleek studio with white walls—something out of a movie. She'd imagined a long divan, upon which she would recline, watching Adam's eyes become inflamed with lust. The easel would topple and he'd ravish her. Ha ha.

In the harsh light of day, she felt no attraction whatsoever. And she wouldn't want to roll around on all those newspapers anyway. For a moment, she considered changing her mind about sitting for Adam and walking out the door. But then he offered her a joint to help her relax and she thought, why not?

22

From her corner of the stage at The Cave, Harumi could see the undulation of bodies. She could pick out the ones who moved to her rhythm. These people weren't like the drunken teenagers of the keg parties on Lake Murray. They didn't show up just for the beer; they wanted to be moved by the music.

Here, the crowd was fevered, in tune with every note she played. They weren't the type to fake their enthusiasm. If they didn't like a band, they'd retreat to the Pink Room or move on to the next club. For the first time in over a year, Harumi felt that old joy. She arched and twisted in response to her own playing. She smiled as Trudy stalked across the floor, hair falling into her face, mic dragging after her.

Trudy was doing the Diana Ross shtick, screaming out the words to Alan's frenzied back beat. Harumi didn't understand Trudy's fascination with the Motown sound. All they sang about back then was getting boyfriends, and Trudy seemed to want the whole world. But she decided to sing these songs, and it was her band, so they played along.

Anyone who listened and watched would know that Trudy was in control. The stage was her little kingdom, and the crowd, throwing their bodies around in the mosh pit below, was in her thrall.

Cassie strummed on the other side of the stage. Harumi could hear the mistakes she made, but no one else seemed to notice. Her fingers were flying over the strings, and Harumi could picture the teeth biting into her lower lip, the crease between her eyebrows that she always had when she was in deep concentration.

At the end of the song Trudy was tossing her hair like an angry horse and flinging her arms all over the place.

"Okay. I'm going to be nice now," Trudy shouted, her voice ragged from use. "I'm going to let Cassie sing because, damn, I'm tired."

Harumi waited while Cassie handed over the guitar. She looked out into the club, smiled at all the sweaty, crazy people. Then, there in the back, she thought she saw someone familiar. It was just a momentary flash of recognition, almost subconscious. She didn't have time to analyze it because Trudy was ready to go on.

It didn't matter if Cassie had psyched herself up yet for the moment or not. This was Trudy's show and they all knew that. As soon as Trudy's hand hit the strings, they were off into "Crashbaby."

Harumi kept her eyes on Cassie. They'd played this song over and over in Trudy's living room. Among themselves, Cassie danced like a barefoot princess on hot coals, but out here, she seemed shy, stage struck. Her voice squeaked a little and the vibe from the audience was uneasy.

"Let it out, girl," Harumi called from her corner, surprising even herself.

And then Cassie closed her eyes and began stomping her combat boots. "*Do you think I'm pretty? Do you wish that you were me?*" She was awesome, naked in her pain.

Harumi was watching Cassie. She didn't see her father until he was up on the stage. She sensed the crowd's attention shifting, and then she looked away from Cassie and saw him, too.

His suit was rumpled from the heat and his hair, usually so carefully pomaded, was roughed up. On his face was an expression Harumi had never seen before—a mix of shame, bitterness, sorrow, and anger. He looked deranged. Harumi wondered if he was drunk.

She kept playing, not knowing what else to do, even after the others stopped. Then his hand was squeezing her arm, tight enough to bruise, and he was pulling her, saying, "Come on. You're coming with me."

Harumi tried to hold her ground, but rage had made him strong. She was no match for his force.

"Hey, old man," a skinhead up front, a huge guy with tattooed biceps and a nose ring, was springing onto the stage. "Get your hands off her!"

Harumi saw the guy's hand clamp over her father's shoulder and she knew what would happen. Her father would be punched and battered and tossed out into the street. People would spit on him and hurl racial slurs.

"It's okay," Harumi said quietly. The thought of a riot made her feel sick to her stomach. "He's my dad."

She unslung her bass and laid it on the stage. Trudy and the others would take care of it later. For now, she would leave with her father. She had never been so humiliated in her life.

"Sorry about this," she said to her friends.

"Are you going to be okay?" Trudy asked in a low voice.

"Yeah." She nodded quickly to Cassie. "I'll call you both tomorrow."

The club was silent, everyone engaged in this unexpected drama. As Harumi and her father stepped down, the onlookers parted, and the two of them walked out together. When they reached the stairwell, a buzz of conversation started up. Harumi could hear Trudy saying, "Hey, sorry about that. Does anyone here know how to play the bass?"

On the way home, Harumi's father didn't speak. Harumi was glad. She needed some time to organize her thoughts and prepare her defense. A part of her wanted to jump out of the car at the red light, run away, and never come back. She didn't think she would ever be able to explain to her parents what the band meant to her. The way it made her feel. She could hardly explain it to herself. All she knew was that she was finally in the world, released from that hothouse existence that had been her childhood, and she wanted to stay where she was.

Her mother was sitting on the sofa when they walked in the door. She held herself erect. Her face was blank. Koji was there, too. He looked up when Harumi entered the room. He, of all people, knew what she was in for.

"Sit down," her father said.

Harumi sat on a footstool with her back straight. She wanted to fall into the chintz-covered chair and kick off her shoes, but she knew that her comfort would irritate them more.

"*Watashi wa totemo hazukashii*," her mother said.

Here we go. Harumi sighed. *The shame, the humiliation, the loss of face.* What did they expect of her anyhow? Did they want her to study tea ceremony and flower arrangement?

"We have been patient," her mother went on. "We listened to that doctor and we waited for you to get better. But you have turned into the worst kind of daughter." Her voice broke, and she brought a hand to her mouth.

"You are going to college and study music," her father said. "We learned that you haven't applied to the universities as we hoped, so you may have to start one semester late. In the meantime, I will give you a job in my company. You will do typing and such for the other architects."

"Do you have my husband picked out for me, too?" Harumi couldn't help herself. She prepared herself for a slap across the face.

But her father didn't seem to have any energy left for violence. "Your insolence is intolerable," he said through clenched teeth.

"I don't know what you're thinking," Harumi said. "I'm eighteen. An adult. I can do whatever I want."

"No, you can't. You are still our daughter. You will always be our daughter and everything you do reflects upon this family."

Harumi had heard stories of old Japan. Stories about wayward girls who had wrecked their families' fortunes. Or the one about the beautiful leper girl who was banished to an island far away because her sickness would taint the whole family. Her siblings weren't able to marry. No one would shop at her father's store. Harumi thought her parents were living out some kind of samurai story, clinging to modes of behavior that had probably become obsolete in the land of their birth.

No one in America would think less of her if she were in a rock band. Probably no one in Japan, either. Things had changed since her mom was a girl. The neighbors must have thought her perverse for spending so many years playing the violin. Harumi remembered hearing Esther's mother cluck her tongue and say, "This is your childhood. Tell your parents that you need to have fun." Who were they keeping up appearances for, anyway?

23

Cassie barged into the house with her guitar banging against her hip. "Hey, I'm home," she called out. She'd seen the sports car in the driveway and knew that one of them was there.

It was Johnette. She was sitting on the sofa with a pile of wadded tissues in front of her. A box of chocolates sat on the coffee table. Half of them had been eaten.

"Umm, is something wrong?" Cassie didn't want to get involved with Johnette's problems, but she couldn't think of anything else to say, considering the circumstances.

"Hi, honey." Johnette sniffed loudly, then patted her tear-streaked face with a fresh tissue. "You got a minute? Can you talk?"

Cassie set the guitar against the wall. "What's up?"

"I think—I think your daddy is having an affair."

Already? "Why do you say that?"

"Someone—and I'm not going to say who—saw him in a hotel lounge when he was supposed to be working late."

"So?" Cassie could feel a headache coming on. She resisted an urge to jump up for aspirin.

"So, number one, he lied to me. And number two, he was with someone. A woman."

"Maybe it was his secretary and they were working late in the hotel lounge." Cassie had heard of men who were incapable of fidelity. It was wired into them or something. She didn't know the details of her father's sex life, of course, but she wondered if he was some kind of addict like President Kennedy.

"No, no. This woman had on a low-cut dress. Her hand was on his thigh."

What was she, some kind of marriage counselor? Was it her job to warn off her father's lovers? *Don't marry this man. He'll cheat on you.*

"Well, are you sure it was Daddy? You ought to ask him directly. It might be some huge mix-up."

Johnette started crying. She covered her face with her hands and Cassie saw that her nail polish was chipped. Her hair was oily, too, as if she'd given up on bathing. She began rocking, her keening rising to the ceiling.

Cassie felt dizzy all of a sudden. Johnette's crying was getting all mixed up with her mother's voice. She could hear Mama yelling, "You bitch. You whore. You home wrecker." She could hear the ice clinking in her mama's glass. Sobs. Screams. The squeal of tires.

"I'm sorry," Cassie murmured, gripping her head. Drills were biting into her brain. The living room went blurry. She ran for the door, knocking over a basket of laundry on the way. The door was so heavy, but she managed to push it open. Johnette was calling after her. She didn't turn back. She rested on the front porch for a moment, sucking in fresh air, until the pain subsided. Slowly, everything came back into focus—the black mailbox at the end of the driveway, the birdbath centered on the lawn, the brick house across the street. Then she got into her car and drove away.

Where to go? She stopped by Trudy's house, but no one was home. Esther and Harumi were both at work. She kept driving till she found herself in front of Adam's house.

When he opened the door, she thought she had the wrong place. All surfaces—the tables and counters and chairs—were cleared. The floors, too, were spick and span and free of clutter.

"What happened here?" Cassie asked, throwing herself on the sofa. "Did you hire a maid?"

Adam laughed. "No, my parents came to visit."

How weird to imagine Adam with parents. It was even stranger to realize that he cared what they thought of his lifestyle and that he was willing to clean up for them. They must all be close.

Cassie had never tried to impress her daddy with housekeeping. They'd had someone come in twice a week to run the vacuum over the plush carpets and dust the tables for as long as she could remember. Even if she had cleaned her own room, it's not like Daddy would have noticed. He didn't really give a damn about what Cassie did or didn't do.

Back when she was fifteen, he'd come across Cassie and a boy both naked in the den. Instead of going for the shotgun like a normal father, he'd turned red and excused himself. The boy had fled the house with his shirt untucked and his shoes untied. Cassie had waited and waited for a reprimand or at least a chat about safe sex, but the issue never came up.

In this cleaned-up room, even Adam looked better. His skin had more color. He was wearing a white cotton shirt and faded jeans. His hair had been trimmed.

"Do you want a drink?" Adam asked. "Smoke some pot?"

At first Cassie had thought that she wanted to talk, but now it didn't seem worth the bother. Plus, if she mentioned Johnette, her stepmother would always be between them, shared knowledge hovering like a spirit. She just wanted to be oblivious for a while. "No, thanks." She crooked her finger at him.

Adam grinned. He pulled the blinds, and the room became darker, like twilight. Then he prowled toward her, a cat going after a bird.

Cassie stayed still, watching him with amusement. When he was within her reach, she yanked him toward her by his belt loops. He lost his balance and fell on top of her.

Cassie squirmed out from underneath and straddled his hips. She began unbuttoning his shirt, leaning down to kiss his brown nipples. When she got to the last button, she tried to slide it over his shoulders.

He sat up to help her out, wriggling out of his shirt and attacking her buttons at the same time. When his arms were bared, Cassie sucked in her breath. The soft insides of his elbows were black with bruises. Track marks. He was a junkie.

Maybe she should have been repelled, but she wasn't in a way. It was cool. A turn-on. It made him seem tragic and dangerous, like Jim Morrison or Billie Holiday. She wondered what it would be like to stick a needle in her veins. Just once.

24

Harumi watched the taillights of the taxi until they were out of sight, then heaved her suitcase and bass case onto the porch. She could hear Diana Ross belting out "I Hear a Symphony." Trudy was home.

She banged on the door, but no one came. Finally she tried the doorknob. It was open. She waited till the song died down and stuck her head inside. "Hey, Trudy?"

A few seconds later, she popped out of her room. "Harumi!" A smile lit up her face. "What's up?"

"Can I crash here for a few nights? My dad went psycho. He's about to lock me in the attic—without Zelda—and throw away the key. I had to get out of there."

"Yeah, I know how parents can be. I've sent mine invitations to all of our gigs so far, and they haven't shown up once." Trudy grabbed the suitcase by the handle and started dragging it into the middle of the room. "My new motto is 'Make Your Own Family.' So welcome, sister. The sofa is yours."

"Thanks." Harumi sank into the cushions. She was suddenly overcome with exhaustion. Well, tomorrow was Saturday. Maybe she could sleep in. "I owe you one."

Trudy disappeared for a moment. Harumi thought she was off to get sheets and a pillow, but no. She returned with two bottles of beer and her guitar.

"I want to learn to play this thing for real. Could you give me some pointers while you're here?"

Really, all Harumi wanted was to curl up on that plaid acrylic and go to sleep, but she didn't want to be rude. Trudy was being really nice and she had to respect her desire to become a better musician. A lot of people thought that Trudy was just fooling around, but Harumi knew that she was totally serious about the band and their music.

"Yeah, okay." Harumi rubbed her eyes and straightened up. "Get ready for lesson one."

The look on Trudy's face was pure bliss. "Oh, thank you, thank you."

Harumi had to admit that it was nice to be appreciated.

The next morning, after four hours of sleep, Harumi woke to the crashing of pots and pans.

"I hate you!" It was Madeline, Trudy's apartment-mate.

"What are you doing? You're going to take my head off with that thing." Harumi guessed it was Madeline's boyfriend speaking.

"That's the point!"

And then came the sound of a cast-iron frying pan thudding on the floor.

Harumi's head hurt. She wanted to ask Gil to turn down the stereo. The jazz was making everything worse. It was weird in a way, a musician craving silence. But music wasn't the problem. It was a lack of sleep, an overabundance of stress. After spending the last few nights on Trudy's sofa, she knew that she had to find another place to live, and fast.

All she could afford with her tips from Goatfeathers was a little attic room somewhere. Or maybe she could find roommates who were a little less dramatic. There was no way she was going back home with her tail between her legs.

Harumi saw Chip come in through the door. He loosened his tie as he made his way to his favorite stool. Goatfeathers was like his living room or something. Harumi wondered what his real living room looked like. His cuffs and collars were always neatly pressed, his trousers expertly creased. He seemed the type of guy who'd fold his old newspapers and stack them in a corner for recycling. He'd have a great stereo system, and a leather modular sofa and thick cream-colored carpet to cushion every step.

All right, she was projecting. She was imagining the opposite of Trudy's apartment because that's what she craved at the moment. In reality, she knew next to nothing about Chip. She knew that he was a stockbroker, and that he liked Red Stripe and Sapporo beer, and, sometimes, chips with guacamole dip. He probably worked out, because she could see that he had muscular forearms when he rolled back his sleeves and he didn't have a gut hanging over his waistband like a lot of post-college grads. She figured he was close to thirty. His brown hair was just beginning to recede, but he was basically a handsome guy.

He smelled good, too. Harumi caught a whiff of his citrusy cologne when she got close to the table. "Hey, Chip. The usual?"

He looked up from his magazine and smiled. "Naw. I think I'll try something different today. Bring me a Tsing Tao."

"Coming up." Harumi felt a little bit better now that Chip was here. She knew he'd leave a good tip and he was unfailingly polite, unlike the frat boys who often crowded in. Plus, he was obviously a guy in control of his destiny, and after all of the disorder of the past week or so, that was somehow reassuring.

She took a bottle of the Chinese beer out of the refrigerator, pulled a chilled mug from the freezer, and put them both on a tray. When she was arranging the cocktail napkin at Chip's elbow, he said, "So do you work all the time? Or do you get a night off?"

Harumi kept her eyes on the beer bottle. "I get time off."

"Would you be interested in having dinner with me?"

Harumi froze for a moment, then hurried to finish her business. She set down the frosted mug with a little more force than she'd intended. "I don't know," she said. "I'm in a band. We have to practice a lot."

"I see."

Harumi looked at him then. He was trying to smile, but his eyes flickered away from hers. She'd embarrassed him. Oh, no. "Do you want some peanuts or something? A piece of cheesecake?"

"No, thanks."

She lingered for a moment longer, but he just nodded and picked up the magazine he'd been thumbing through earlier. There goes my tip, she thought. She slunk behind the counter and started to mop up imaginary spills.

No one had ever asked her out before. She wouldn't even know what to do on a date. Chip probably thought that she was blowing him off, or that she had a boyfriend stashed away somewhere, but really, she was scared. She wanted to tell him this. She even thought of writing a message on the back of his check, but Gil asked her to do something in the stock room, and when she'd finished arranging bottles on the shelves, Chip's stool was empty and two dollars were on the table.

Harumi picked up the money and studied it for a moment. It was just ordinary money, of course, George Washington and a pyramid with an eye, but she folded it and stuffed it into her skirt pocket instead of stuffing it into the tip jar to be divided evenly among the members of the wait staff. It was silly, she knew, junior high school behavior, but suddenly Chip was a looming presence in her life.

A couple came into Goatfeathers, a guy with long blond hair in a crisp white shirt with his mini-skirted date. They crawled into a booth, both on the same side, so they could sit thigh to thigh. Harumi watched them, watched their fingers grapple and cling under the table. They were so easy with one another, so possessive of one another's bodies. Was this behavior natural? Harumi tried to imagine sitting like that with Chip. She imagined him brushing the hair from her ear and whispering against her skin.

She brought a menu to the couple, but they barely noticed her. They were locked in their own world. Harumi remembered a story her mother had told her about an invisible string connecting the little fingers of those who were fated to be lovers. She looked at the young woman's pinky. It was long and slender, and now it was in the blond guy's mouth.

"I'll be back in a minute," Harumi said. She didn't think they were paying attention.

When the last of the customers had disappeared and her shift had ended, Gil offered her a ride home on the back of his motorcycle.

"No, that's okay. But thanks." She knew it wasn't safe to wander the streets at one A.M., but a walk home would give her a few minutes of solitude. She needed a bit of peace before walking back into Trudy's realm.

The stars were dimmed by clouds. Harumi dragged her feet, kicking up pebbles. From the yard, she could hear the blare of a Supremes record. She sat on the edge of the porch, trying to build up enough energy to get through the door. Trudy would probably spew advice freely, if asked, but Harumi had already heard the stories—how she'd spent time in the juvenile home, how she'd set Adam's room on fire. Trudy's life was a mess, and Harumi didn't want to model her love life after hers. She'd have to play it by ear.

25

Esther had been stuck at school with a teacher who wanted to discuss her paper, and now she was thirty minutes late for work. She thought of popping into a phone booth and letting Rebecca know she was on her way, but figured she'd be better off heading straight for the gallery.

A sneaky part of her knew that Rebecca wouldn't yell at her or dock her pay for tardiness, but Esther tried not to abuse her privileges; she wanted to keep everything professional at work.

When she walked in the door, she was surprised to find Rebecca in her path, tapping her toes with her arms crossed. "Where have you been?" She pointed to her watch, and then, for emphasis, to the clock on the wall, an arty timepiece with arrows for hands and shapes instead of numbers.

"Sorry," Esther said, ducking her head. Rebecca was obviously agitated and it was obviously her fault, but why?

"I've got something to tell you."

Esther looked up then and saw that Rebecca wasn't angry, just impatient.

"What is it you've always wanted?" Rebecca asked in a gentle, coaxing voice.

Esther had no idea where this was leading. She tossed up her hands. "A million dollars? World peace?"

"Be serious, dear." Rebecca rested her hands on Esther's shoulders and leaned in to deliver her message. "I've made you a drummer."

"What?"

"That's what you wanted, isn't it? To be a drummer for Screaming Divas."

Esther rubbed her forehead with her palm. This made no sense. She was still in the floundering-around-in-the-basement stage. She wasn't ready to join the band yet, and she hadn't auditioned. "What did you do?"

"Well, Trudy—Ms. Sin, rather—came by earlier and asked me to handle bookings for the band . . . ."

Esther sighed. "And you said you'd do it if they let me be drummer."

Rebecca's arms dropped to her side and she took a few paces. "Not *let.* I didn't say 'let.'"

Esther could feel tears welling, but she fought them back. She wanted to be in control of her own life, but Rebecca had the reins. At the very least, she could control her emotions.

"Rebecca," she said flatly. "I appreciate everything you do for me, but I wanted to do just this one thing on my own."

"But she asked me," Rebecca went on. "She begged me to help them and then she told me that they need a new drummer and I thought of you. If you don't want to do it, I'll find somebody else."

Esther climbed onto the stool behind the cash register and leaned on her elbows. What was it that her mother was always saying? It's not what you know, it's who you know. And she knew Rebecca. She had to admit that her mentor was well connected and willing to make things happen. If it took Rebecca's intervention to get close to Harumi and Cassie, then she'd put up with it.

"All right. I'm sorry I overreacted." Esther took a deep breath and forced a smile. "It is what I want, but I'm nervous. I'm not sure I can live up to their—and your—expectations. I've only been practicing for a couple of weeks."

Rebecca approached her then. She wrapped her arms around Esther and murmured into her hair. "I know that you'll be fabulous. No one will be disappointed."

Then the door whooshed open and Esther wriggled out of her embrace.

26

Christmas was coming. Cassie dreaded the thought. She couldn't imagine anything worse than sitting around a fake tree with Johnette's low-fat candy cane cookies. Or maybe Johnette wouldn't be there. Cassie was putting off the rest of her Christmas shopping till she found out what the deal with her father and stepmother was. She'd already bought gifts for the Divas: for Trudy, an LP of *The Supremes Live at the Copacabana*, earrings shaped like guitars for Harumi, and a book of poetry for Esther. She'd gotten her dad a sweater—cashmere, no less—but she didn't want to waste money on Johnette's present if she was about to move out.

Cassie stopped wondering when her dad called her into his office.

"Listen, Cass, I need to talk to you about Christmas." He was all business, no time for small talk. "I hate to do this to you, but I'm not going to be around."

"You're not?"

"Johnette and I, well, we've been having some problems that we need to work out, so I've promised her we'd go somewhere, just the two of us."

"I get it, Daddy. You don't have to apologize." Cassie tried to keep joy from sneaking into her voice. "I think that's a great idea."

"You do? Well, I'm glad you're so understanding. We'll bring you back something nice."

They were headed for the Virgin Islands. They'd be cruising in and out of ports, buying trinkets in duty-free shops, dancing to reggae on the deck. And Cassie wouldn't have to endure another "family" Christmas.

"I'll drive you up to Aunt Belle's house, if you like. I'm sure they'd love to have you."

"No, that's okay. A friend invited me to spend Christmas with her family," she quickly improvised. She wasn't in the mood for Aunt Belle and her sympathy. She'd stay with Trudy. Then again, Trudy might be spending some time with her dad. Maybe she'd just stay home and spend her evenings watching all those holiday specials on TV like *Frosty the Snowman* and *How the Grinch Stole Christmas*.

"Don't worry about me, Daddy. I'll be fine."

"Good, good." He liked having a low maintenance daughter, Cassie thought. Especially since his wives and lovers were anything but.

"So what do you want for Christmas?" he asked.

At first, she was going to say "nothing," but then she realized that this was an opportunity. He was feeling guilty, which meant he would be generous. Maybe generous enough to fund Screaming Divas' first demo.

"Well, there is one thing . . . ." she began.

When they were finished talking, she went into her room and sat on the edge of her bed, trying to think up a good gift for Johnette. And for Adam. She wasn't sure that buying a present for him was appropriate. After all, he wasn't exactly her boyfriend. He was more like an addiction. The more she had of him, the more she needed him. Maybe that's how her mother had felt about booze. Maybe she'd inherited a personality disorder.

Cassie wondered what it would be like to have been brought up in a normal family—like the Shealys, say. According to Esther, they played Scrabble by the hearth and her mother made casseroles with canned soup. What a life. It would be a hoot to have just a day of that.

27

Harumi had a new home—an apartment in the Shandon area of Five Points, an upscale neighborhood of well-kept brick buildings with magnolia trees in the front yard. She'd moved in with a widow who needed caretaking. The widow's daughter, a brisk woman with a catering business, had interviewed her in her paneled office. The questions had been personal ("Do you have a boyfriend?" "Have you ever used drugs?"), but Harumi knew the woman was just looking out for her mother and tried not to take offense.

Rent was cheap—a hundred dollars a month—but Harumi had to prepare the old lady's meals and run errands for her. She was supposed to do housework, too, and whatever else came up—stuff that would make her upwardly mobile mother cringe.

The night before, the woman, Mrs. Harris, had called Harumi into her bedroom. She was propped against the padded headboard of her bed, wearing a pink flannel nightgown scattered with rosebuds. Wisps of white hair floated over her shoulders. Her vision was poor and when Harumi walked in, Mrs. Harris moved her head at the sound, but seemed to be staring just to the left of her ear.

"Darling, would you read to me?"

Harumi looked at her watch. She was supposed to be at band practice in an hour. If she were late, Trudy would probably blow a gasket and threaten to kick her out of the band. Trudy rarely acted on her threats, but Harumi didn't want to deal with another of her tantrums.

On the other hand, she couldn't refuse Mrs. Harris, whom she'd started thinking of as her benefactor. She imagined the woman had pots of money set aside and that if she, Harumi, was loyal, Mrs.

Harris would write her into her will. If she was lucky, the woman would fall asleep to the drone of her voice.

"Okay, Mrs. Harris. I'll read to you."

A leather-bound Bible was on the nightstand and Harumi figured she'd be reading psalms, but Mrs. Harris pointed a shaky finger at her dresser against the wall. "Look in the top drawer, dear," she said. "My book's in there."

Harumi yanked on the brass latch and looked down at the piles of big, white underpants.

"At the bottom," Mrs. Harris said. "I've hidden it." She giggled.

Harumi hesitated, then pushed aside the mounds of stretched, stained nylon and found a dog-eared paperback. On the cover, a pirate held a half-naked woman in his arms. "Um, *Galley Wench*? Is this it?"

Mrs. Harris clapped her hands together and sighed like a girl at a party. "Yesssss."

Harumi shoved the drawer shut and perched on the edge of the bed. "Uh, what page are you on?"

"Read page one hundred seventy-six. That's my favorite." Her hands were still clasped at her chest.

Harumi cleared her throat. "She wriggled in his arms, but could not free herself. 'Be still woman,' he said. 'I've waited too long for this.'" Harumi could feel a blush shading her cheeks, but Mrs. Harris didn't notice. She couldn't see what was in the room, but she was obviously picturing the pirate and the wench, the pirate's big strong hands tearing the wench's dress apart. Mrs. Harris was enraptured by the muscle-roped thighs of the hero, the shining tumescence of his member. She wasn't about to fall asleep.

Harumi continued reading until the characters were in their clothes again. Then she paused long enough for Mrs. Harris to say, "Thank you, dear. That was wonderful." She put the book back in its hiding place, and eased herself out of the room.

Walking to Trudy's house with Zelda in her arms, she still felt embarrassed. She had a vivid picture in her head of the lovers in the book. But then it melted into a vision of her and Chip. Chip, unbuttoning her blouse. Chip's tongue in her mouth.

She hadn't seen him since that night he'd asked her out. She was beginning to think he'd never visit Goatfeathers again.

Mrs. Harris had urges at unreasonable hours that Harumi did her best to fulfill.

"Darling, do you know what I would like?"

Mrs. Harris was sitting in her favorite rocking chair, listening to a drama on TV.

Harumi braced herself. She'd seen that dreamy look before. "Uh, no. What can I get you?"

"I would like a bowl of vanilla ice cream with three or four fresh strawberries on the side."

Harumi released her breath. This was a possibility. There was no ice cream in the freezer, but she could jog over to the Food Lion and make this woman's wish come true.

"I can do that, Mrs. Harris. You wait right there, and I'll go out and get you some ice cream."

Harumi slipped on a pair of sandals, grabbed her wallet, and headed out the door. It was just after ten and the air was cool and fresh. She raised her face to the night.

Food Lion was a couple of blocks away. At the corner, a murky figure leapt out at her. "Boo!"

Harumi jumped. Then she saw the buzz-cut ROTC guy, and relaxed. "Geez. Leave me alone."

The guy barked a laugh and she caught a whiff of liquor. In the morning, he'd wake up next to a dumpster and wonder where he was.

Harumi stepped up her pace and pushed past him.

He trailed her for a block. She could hear the syncopation of footsteps behind her, his shuffle and stumble. The hairs at the back of her neck rose like antennae. He was probably harmless, but she wanted peace. She wanted to inhale jasmine, bathe in the moonlight. Suddenly she stopped and whirled. "Stop following me."

"Hey, it's a free country." She couldn't see his face. There was only that twangy, taunting voice. "Ah kin walk wherever ah want." He moved closer in the dark.

Harumi took a step backward.

He lunged at her and she felt a vise clamp around her upper arm. She felt the heat of his body along the length of her own.

"Get away from me." Now her voice was shrill. "I'll scream."

His grip loosened and she wrenched herself free, turned, and started running. When she reached Devine Street, with its chain of traffic, she paused and looked behind her. He was gone.

The grocery store was almost empty. Wives had already been in and out. At this hour, the only shoppers were students with the munchies and singles dropping in after work.

The fluorescent lights were a relief after that encounter in the street. Here, everything was clean and safe. Harumi wandered into the produce department for strawberries.

"Hey." Another voice behind her, but this one was familiar.

"Chip."

The sight of him was so comforting that she felt like hugging him. He was wearing his blue Oxford shirt and pushing a shopping cart. Harumi couldn't help looking down into the wire cage: a slab of steak, a jug of low-fat milk, lettuce, a case of Coors, a papaya.

"Dinner?" she asked.

"Yeah. You?"

"Strawberries." Then she laughed. She told him about Mrs. Harris and her sudden desire for ice cream. And then, because she could tell he was enjoying her story, she told him about *Galley Wench*.

Chip slapped his hand to his forehead and laughed. When he calmed down, he reached for a package of strawberries and said, "What time does she go to bed?" He gestured to the case of beer in his cart. "Do you think you could slip out and join me for dinner Friday night?"

Harumi smiled, feeling suddenly mischievous. "Maybe."

Together, they went to the freezer section, picked out ice cream, and went through the checkout. Then Chip led Harumi to his car. "I can't believe you walk around here by yourself at night," he said, his forehead wrinkling. "It's not safe."

Harumi shrugged, then shivered.

Chip was staring at her. He caught that look of fear and quickly opened the passenger side door of his Saab. "Are you cold?"

His voice was gentle, soft as a pillow. She wanted to lean against him, but got into the car instead.

During a break at band practice the next afternoon, Harumi spoke up. "Hey, y'all?"

Esther put down her drumsticks, and Cassie laid her guitar on the sofa. Suddenly all eyes were on Harumi. They looked eager, like hungry puppies, and she knew that they expected her to say something about their music, like they were waiting for some genius suggestion to come out of her mouth. But she surprised them.

"I need your advice."

Esther's eyes bugged out. Cassie's jaw dropped, and Trudy leaned in closer. "On what?"

"I met this guy at Goatfeathers," Harumi started. Her eyes met Esther's. Of all people, Esther knew what a sheltered life she'd led up till now. "And I'm going out with him for the first time on Friday night."

"That's great!" Cassie said.

"Yeah," Trudy chimed in. "We weren't going to have practice that day, anyway."

Harumi could feel her skin burning. "No, I mean, I've never gone out with a guy before. This is my *first time.* I don't even know what to wear. And should I, you know, let him *kiss me*?"

For a moment, they were all stunned into silence.

Finally, Cassie said, "I've got a dress that would look great on you."

Today, Cassie was wearing a black T-shirt with a shredded hem over a white tank top. Gaps in her jeans were held together with safety pins.

"He's not punk," Harumi clarified. "He's older, in his twenties. He has a job . . . ."

"What does he do?" Trudy asked.

At first, Harumi considered lying. She worried that these friends of hers, with their artists and musicians, wouldn't understand the appeal of a guy like Chip who wore a new Armani suit to work, as opposed to something from the Salvation Army. But she had no one else to turn to.

"He's a stockbroker."

Again, they were rendered speechless. It was as if, with her words, she'd cut off their tongues. Then she heard Esther clear her throat. "He'll probably take you someplace nice, then. So you'll want to dress up."

28

Cassie sat on the edge of Esther's mind like an angel, a muse, and when she got home from band practice, she often found herself feeling around for a pen and scribbling down poetry. She would write a song, she decided. She would prove to them that she was worthy of being in the band, that she was willing to work hard at every aspect of being a musician.

Even though she couldn't read music and could barely tap out a beat with her drumsticks, she could hum. While she was driving to work she would sometimes turn down the radio and sing out one of her own creations. She wasn't sure how she'd ever get up the courage to present her lyrics to the group. Cassie wrote lots of songs, but Trudy was quick to shoot them down when she was in a bad mood.

One afternoon, after they'd played their standards for what seemed to be the millionth time, Trudy grabbed her hair in clumps and bared her teeth. "Grrr. I'm so sick of these same damn songs. If we don't come up with something new, I think I'm gonna shoot myself."

For a few seconds, the others froze. Cassie set her mouth in a hard line. Harumi's eyes dropped to the soiled carpet. Esther watched Trudy's face, trying to work up some nerve.

Finally, she took a deep breath and cleared her throat. "Um, as a matter of fact, I've written a few songs myself."

Trudy looked at her. "Really?"

"Um, yeah." Esther put down her drumsticks and pulled a notebook out of her backpack. She flicked past the notes from her Southern Lit class and tore a page from the notebook. "Here." Her heart was trying to get out of her chest.

Trudy snatched the paper and read out loud:

"Last night I had the craziest dream
You were waltzing in a moonbeam.
When you got close you reached out to me
And said, 'Come on, let's dance. We'll be free.'

"We share the same blood
We're sisters under the skin.
Rise out of the mud
Our love is no sin.

"Last night you whispered into my hair
'Kiss me right now, if you dare.'
I closed my eyes and welcomed your lips
And until morning I took little sips.

"I pray for the night
Because that's when we meet
I hate the daylight
Reality is not as sweet
As the dreams where I hear you say

"'We share the same blood
We're sisters under the skin
Rise out of the mud
Our love is no sin.'"

When Trudy had finished she glanced over at Harumi, whose neck still drooped, then Cassie, who was watching Esther. Finally she aimed her eyes at Esther and sneered, "This is Hallmark crap. We can't sing this." She thrust the paper back at Esther. "We're *bitches*. Don't you get it?" She snorted and tossed her head.

"It could be a ballad," Cassie said. "I think it's kind of pretty, especially the part about dancing in the moonlight."

Trudy glared at her. "We don't do ballads. We're punk."

Cassie shrugged. It was obvious that Trudy was in one of her moods and there weren't going to be any drastic changes in her point of view in the next few minutes.

Esther crumpled the paper and stuffed it into her pocket. Later she'd burn the whole notebook. She kept her face turned away from the others while she packed up her equipment. She'd suffered enough humiliation for one day; she didn't want anyone to see her tears. She felt a gentle hand on her back.

"Hey." It was Cassie.

Esther looked up and sniffled.

"Hey, don't let her get to you. Trudy's mad at the world, not you. She's got all these unresolved issues with her parents. You know, her dad kicked her out of the house and her mama doesn't want to have anything to do with her. Sometimes the anger just jumps out of her."

Esther nodded, but it was hard not to take rejection personally.

"By the way, I think it's a beautiful song."

Esther tried to twist her lips into a smile. Cassie had never been so nice to her before. She knew she'd play this moment over and over while she stared at the ceiling that night.

"If you wait a sec, I'll walk out with you," Cassie whispered.

Esther rubbed the tears out of her eyes and nodded. She wanted to burst out of the house and never go back, but Cassie's sweetness made everything else worthwhile. She lingered by the door while Cassie gathered up her guitar and exchanged a few final wisecracks with Trudy. Then Cassie winked at her, and they left the house together.

Cassie's Beetle was parked right in front, but she walked with Esther to her car across the street.

Esther didn't know why Cassie was walking to her car and she didn't know what to say. They were silent until she slipped the key into the lock.

"It was you, wasn't it?" Cassie's voice was calm and clear.

Esther turned to look at her, a sudden panic tightening her chest. "What?"

"You're the one who wrote me all those letters."

For a second, Esther thought about throwing herself into her car and peeling out of there. Would there be no end to her shame on this awful night? But then she looked into Cassie's eyes and saw nothing but wonder and curiosity. "Yes," she confessed, in a strange, high voice.

Cassie stepped back. "I thought so." She smiled then, as if solving the mystery had given her great joy. "I still have them, you know. They're in a shoebox under my bed." Then Cassie put a finger to her lips and Esther knew that she wouldn't tell anyone. It would be their secret.

Esther watched her retreat. She watched until Cassie had gotten into her car and started the engine. She saw Cassie's hand lift from the steering wheel.

Esther waved back, then sank against the vinyl seats, trying to still her trembling limbs.

29

Cassie knew about Adam's habit, but she'd never seen him shoot up before. She wasn't even sure she'd ever seen him when the junk was coursing through his veins, though there had been afternoons when his eyes were unnaturally bright, his movements a little too slow.

One afternoon when Cassie was sitting cross-legged on his floor, he reached under the tattered sofa for the wooden box that held his kit.

"Can I watch?" she asked, before he had a chance to ask her to leave.

Adam looked at her face for a long moment. Then he dropped his eyes and lifted the lid. "I don't care."

She was silent and still, like a hiker in the presence of wildlife. She watched his ritual—the careful measuring of white powder, the spoon over the flame, the belt tightened over his bicep—with fascination. And then she observed the needle sliding into his vein, the backwash of blood in the syringe, the relaxation of his face. He moaned, then fell back against the sofa, forgetting she was there.

It scared her as much as it attracted her. She knew how easily things could go wrong, yet she craved that instant relief. She'd thought all this time that she wanted only to be loved, but what she really wanted was to get out of her body.

The next time she went to him, she asked if she could try, too.

He grinned crookedly, his unwashed hair falling in his eyes. "What? You want me to corrupt you?"

"It's too late for that," she said.

He stared at her for a long time and she was afraid that he'd see the desperation there. She should try to be more casual about it. Make it seem like it didn't matter to her at all.

Finally his gaze dropped. "All right."

Cassie smiled.

"You have to be careful," he told her, as he tapped out the powder. "You shouldn't do this alone. And never when drunk. People pass out and choke on their own vomit. Got it?"

She nodded, flipped her hair back. She hated being babied. She probably knew more about the world than Adam, with his ordinary middle class parents and interior trips. Heroin didn't make you wise. Or at least she didn't expect it to.

She held out her arm, the way she did for nurses, and waited while he tied a silk scarf around her. The veins popped out, blue and fat. He pressed down on one with his finger, then kissed it. Cassie thought it was the most erotic thing he'd ever done.

She closed her eyes, heard him tapping the ampoule with a fingernail, then felt the needle's prick.

She waited for something to happen.

At first, there was nothing, and then gradually, she felt a calm enter her body. It was like being in the warm bath water with Mama, having her head stroked as she drifted off to sleep, or being rocked, maybe. It was lovely, like a Monet watercolor, blurry and soft.

But that first afternoon, she wound up cramped and retching over the toilet. Adam, seemingly unaffected, held her torso and smoothed back her hair.

"The first time can be rough," he said. He kissed her clammy cheek. "Believe me, it gets better."

She vowed she would try again.

30

Friday evening, Harumi stood in front of the mirror in Cassie's leopard print sheath. It looked odd on her, like a costume, but there was nothing in her own closet that seemed right. She'd changed three times already—from a red silk dress (too Chinese) to a Laura Ashley floral ensemble (too prim) to a tunic and black tights (too Goatfeathers; he'd already seen it twenty times). Cassie was the daughter of a beauty queen. She knew more about dressing up than anyone. Harumi decided to trust her judgment.

She closed her eyes and thought of Tiffany Hart, heroine of Mrs. H.'s latest romance novel. *Tiffany's voluptuous breasts threatened to spill out of her red silk gown.*

"Harumi?" Mrs. Harris was calling her. She probably wanted ice cream or a bedtime story, and there was no time for that.

She latched a thrift shop rhinestone bracelet onto her wrist and hurried to the bedroom. "What is it, Mrs. Harris?" she asked from the doorway.

Regal as ever, the woman leaned against her pillows. She reached for Harumi. "Come here, my dear."

Harumi's gaze slipped to the clock. Chip was due any minute. She hoped he'd be late.

The woman's grip was surprisingly strong. Her skin felt like washed paper, all soft and wrinkled. "Enjoy yourself, my dear," she said in her quavery voice. "But be home by midnight."

"What?" Harumi couldn't help herself. Mrs. Harris was probably lost in the long ago, confusing her with a daughter, and Harumi was usually cheerful about playing along. But if she wasn't, if she was indeed imposing a curfew on her home helper, Harumi would have to set her straight.

"Mrs. Harris, I am an adult. I am old enough to vote or join the army, and I'm not your child."

The woman's eyes widened at this sudden outburst, but then disappeared in the crinkles of a smile. "There, there. No need to get all worked up." She patted Harumi's hand with her liver-spotted one. "I'm doing you a favor. This is your first date with the young man, is it not?"

Harumi nodded, slightly wary.

"And you have never had a boyfriend."

Harumi opened her mouth to protest. Was it so plain to see? Were words tattooed on her forehead? *Virgin. Never been kissed.* Then she remembered that interview with the old woman's daughter.

"If things get too steamy and you're feeling uncomfortable, just tell him that you have to be home by twelve. And that if you're late, I'll fire you." She winked. "And another thing. Be sure to hold back. These modern girls on TV tell their life stories on the first date, but I'm telling you, men like a little mystery. You know those Godiva chocolates I like so much?"

Harumi nodded, not sure where this was going. Mrs. Harris limited herself to one a day.

"Well, you should think of your charms like a box of bonbons. Dole them out slowly. Let him savor each one and make him want more." The woman bore an expression of ecstasy, presumably thinking about chocolate.

"So, uh, which bonbon do you think I should dole out first?"

Her eyes snapped open. "Well, you could talk about hobbies."

"Hobbies?" Surely not her music. That was her passion, her life. She'd done the newspaper crossword that morning. Did that count?

Mrs. Harris released her hands at last to the chime of the doorbell.

"Oh, no," Harumi muttered under her breath. She went to the front room.

Tiffany threw open the door. "Hiya, big boy. I've been thinking about you all day."

"Um, hi."

He was standing there with an armful of blood-red roses.

"They're gorgeous," she said.

Chip looked her up and down. "So are you."

She could feel his eyes on her back as she turned away from him in search of a vase. She couldn't remember how to walk. Every step felt strange.

In the kitchen, she found a glass pitcher big enough to hold the blossoms. She filled it with tap water and unwrapped the cellophane from the stems.

How was she going to make it through the evening? She'd never been so nervous in her life—not even when she'd soloed for the first time.

"Let me change and I'll be right with you."

"No," Chip said. "You look great. I love that dress."

She raised her eyebrows. "This?" A smile splashed across her face. "It's a rag."

Chip was wearing khakis and a cabled cotton tennis sweater, with topsiders without socks. He looked as if he was about to set out for a polo match or the country club.

"At Goatfeathers, when you're all dressed up, you look so chilly and unapproachable. But like this—" He shrugged. "I don't know. You seem friendly."

"Chilly?" She cocked her hip. The spirit of Tiffany had invaded her body. Or it could have been Cassie. The dress. *I'm flirting*, she realized with a shock. "*Moi?*"

He pushed a hand through his hair, shifted from foot to foot. "It took me weeks—*weeks*—to work up the nerve to ask you out. And then you turned me down."

Harumi smiled. "I told you. I had band practice."

"Yeah, right."

She had to turn away so he wouldn't see her dumb grin. "I'll say goodnight to Mrs. Harris and we can be on our way."

Chip's car radio was tuned to NPR. Harumi settled back against the seat to the swell of an orchestra.

"Paganini," she said absently.

Chip looked from the road to Harumi. "I'm impressed. I thought you were into a different kind of music."

Uh oh. Was that a bonbon? "I listen to classical sometimes. I like different kinds of music. Even *enka.*"

"Enka?"

"Yeah, it's kind of like country and western. Songs about drinking and getting your heart broken. It's popular in Japan."

Chip nodded.

She could tell she was racking up points, but he was getting it all wrong.

Then he looked at her and said, "Is your heart broken, Harumi?"

It was a weird question, way too personal. And what was the answer, anyway? No man had had a chance to stomp on her heart yet, but she was aching all the same. This rift with her family was making her lose sleep. She hoped that Chip would pick up on her vibe and change the subject, but he didn't.

"So, Harumi, is that it? You're pining for some other guy?"

She hated the image. And she never wanted to be like Trudy, starved for the attention of someone who didn't want her. "I've never been dumped by a guy," she said. "Why would I be pining?"

Chip turned away. Now he was probably thinking that she was some sort of femme fatale with a string of scalps nailed above her bed. It was wrong to mislead him like this, but there was so much that she didn't want him to know.

"So what do you feel like eating? Thai? Chinese?"

"Italian," she said.

Chip nodded. "How about Garibaldi's?"

At the restaurant, Chip held open doors and ushered her inside with his palm at the small of her back.

She liked feeling his touch. She wondered what it would be like to fall back into his arms. To kiss him.

They were polite with each other through platters of antipasto and spaghetti carbonara. They were giggling by the second bottle of Chianti, stumbling against each other after cappuccino and tiramisu as they made their way to the car.

"So," Chip said, ramming a key into the ignition. "Do you want to drop by my place for a nightcap? Listen to some jazz?"

Harumi felt a flash of panic. She was too drunk to walk in a straight line. There was no way she'd be able to fend off Chip's advances if he got ideas.

The dashboard clock read 10:16. Still early. Would he believe a 10:30 curfew?

"All right," she said. Her voice was barely audible over the engine. "But I have to be home by midnight, or I'll get fired." She rolled her eyes for effect. "She's quirky that way, Mrs. H., but I have to humor her or I'll lose my job."

"Okay, Cinderella."

She watched his hands on the steering wheel, watched the streetlights slide over his sharp jaw. He was so handsome.

They rolled along in silence until Chip clicked the radio on again. The announcer's mellow tones filled the car with words that she knew: Bach, symphony, violin.

She had told him about the band over dinner. He'd seemed to enjoy her quick sketches of Trudy ("Supremes fanatic"), Cassie ("the southern Sylvia Plath"), and Esther ("child boxing champ"). Silently, she'd wondered how she would explain him to her friends. Southern gentleman? Stick-in-the-mud? Trudy might think he was boring, but she liked his old-fashioned interests, his clean and ironed clothes.

"When's your next show?" he'd asked.

"Next Friday. At The Cave."

She couldn't imagine him among the punk wannabes in their leather and safety pins. He'd be as out of place as her father had been. He might get hurt. Even so, when he hinted that he'd be in the audience, front row, with bells on, Harumi had smiled and said, "I'd like that."

The car was drawing up in front of an apartment building with window boxes and shutters. It wasn't sleek and modern as she'd expected. At least, not from the outside.

Chip bolted out of the car and around to the passenger side before she had a chance to get out. She'd never met a man with manners like his. Her own father still walked in doors ahead of her mother, stubbornly clinging to Eastern ways. He never held out chairs or guided his wife with a hand on her back. And of course, he was so different from the guys at The Cave. Adam and Noel were almost another species.

Harumi stood to the side on the narrow porch while Chip unlocked the door. He reached inside and flicked on a light, adjusted the dimmer switch, and waited for her to enter.

Harumi took in the beige carpet and the brown tweed sofa and armchair. She was impressed by the healthy green leaves of the dieffenbachia and ferns. Her father cultivated bonsai, little trees always kept firmly in check, not allowed to grow. Her mother arranged cut flowers in cold glass vases. Here, however, in Chip's living room, there was life, vigor—evidence of a generous spirit.

"Have a seat," he said. "Is cognac all right?"

"Mmm." Harumi sank into the sofa. Crossed her arms and legs. Uncrossed her arms. Tucked her legs beneath her. Let her head loll against the back of the sofa.

Chip returned with two globes of amber liquor.

Harumi's fingers brushed his—zap!—when he passed the glass to her. She closed her eyes and took a sip. She could feel the other end of the sofa sink as he sat down beside her.

"Harumi, how old are you? I mean, if you don't mind my asking."

Her eyes snapped open. "Eighteen."

She saw Chip shrink away from her and set his drink down. "God, I thought you were older. You seem so self-assured."

Was she too young, now?

"I spent a lot of time around adults as a child," she said. "With my parents' friends." It was a little lie, a tiny lie, but she needed to tell it. Too much honesty would be like riding a raft over rapids. Besides, she'd already given him enough bonbons for the night.

"Do you think your parents would like me?"

Harumi shot him a look and was disarmed by his boyish, earnest expression. "No," she said with a laugh, honest this time. "You not nice Japanese boy."

Chip laughed, and guilt stabbed her in the stomach. It was wrong to make fun of her parents with their funny accents and foreign ways, but she was still angry at them.

Harumi lifted her glass and took a big swallow. The cognac burned her lips and tongue. It blazed down her throat. She started coughing.

"Are you okay?" Chip took the drink from her and patted her on the back.

"It went down the wrong way," she said when her breathing was under control again. She wondered if he could tell how nervous she was. His hand was still on her back, and she was sure he could feel, even through her spine, the frantic beating of her heart.

He didn't say anything. His body was still except for his steady, even breathing. And then, as if he'd been gathering up his forces, he tugged Harumi onto his lap, into the cage of his arms, and he kissed her.

She let her lips go slack under his, let his tongue work its way into her mouth. A fever spread through her limbs and loosened her joints. But then his fingers began traveling over her body, grazing nipple and thigh, and her back went rigid. She forgot to breathe. When his mouth left hers for a moment, she sucked in a great gust of air.

"I'm yours," Tiffany panted, her ample chest heaving with desire. "Take me now before I faint."

Harumi couldn't help it. She started laughing.

Chip backed away. "What's so funny?"

"Nothing. I'm really sorry. I just started thinking about—oh, never mind. I think you'd better take me home."

For a moment, he was silent and she thought that he might refuse. They'd both been drinking a lot. Maybe he couldn't drive. She might have to call a taxi.

Harumi couldn't bear to look at him. She remembered the way his expression had frozen when she'd turned him down for a date. This was worse. She'd followed him to his apartment and accepted a drink. She'd even let him kiss her, and then she'd humiliated him by erupting into a giggle fit while kissing him. The man had pride. He probably would never call her again.

They didn't speak in the car. Harumi let herself out as soon as they reached the curb. She mumbled "Thank you" and then dashed up the sidewalk, into the foyer. She could hear the car's engine idling behind her. When she got up to the apartment, she looked out the window. The Saab was gone.

31

On Friday night, The Cave was packed. You couldn't move without stepping on someone's steel-toed boots. This was what Trudy loved.

The band went onstage at ten and played till midnight, nonstop. They knew each other well now, and their set was seamless. With just a nod from Harumi, or a tilt of the head from Cassie, they decided their next song. When they finally quit, Trudy's throat was raw and sore. She'd been a total banshee.

The crowd started chanting, "Dee-vahs! Dee-vahs!"

Trudy shook her head. "My voice is shot. Cassie, you sing something. I gotta get a drink." And then she stepped off the stage.

The crowd parted and Trudy flushed with pleasure. She floated toward the bar, a big smile plastered across her face. Midway, she felt a tug on her arm. She looked to see a girl with eyes made up like Cleopatra, black hair shaved within an inch.

"Hey, I'm the president of the Screaming Divas fan club," the girl said. "Can I interview you for our newsletter sometime?"

A fan club. Wow. "Sure," Trudy said, trying to act as if this happened all the time. Inside, she wanted to whoop for joy. "Give me a call later."

The girl grinned. "Thanks."

Behind her, on the stage, the band broke into a slow song, one they'd rehearsed only a few times. Cassie's voice flooded the club.

At the bar, Trudy heaved herself onto a stool. She was so tired that she didn't even realize Noel was beside her until his lips brushed her ear.

"Why don't you let her sing more often?" he said. "She has a good voice. And she's pretty."

Trudy shrugged. "She doesn't want to."

Noel shook his head. "I'll bet you're holding her back."

Trudy knew he was baiting her. She took a long swig of Diet Coke and pretended to ignore him. Finally she couldn't resist. "So where's the ball and chain?"

Noel shrugged. "Hell if I know. Gone."

"You mean you broke up?" Trudy felt a war whoop rising within, but she contained herself. Instead of rocketing to the ceiling, she put her hand on his shoulder, pretending to console him.

"Yup. She's insane." Noel shook her hand off and turned to her, all businesslike. "So she's gone, which means that we need a new bass player. What do you say?"

Trudy bit back a grin. This was the moment she'd been dreaming of. I'm a hot commodity, she told herself. *Everybody wants me and it feels great!* So what if her parents couldn't be bothered to see her shows. It was better than booze, better than sex, better than any kind of drug. Then she took a hard look at her band. Cassie was center stage. She was still, but an energy radiated from her and all eyes were on her. Harumi's fingers were acrobatic, her concentration almost supernatural. And Esther pounded out the beat as if her life depended on it. Her red hair was flying all over the place.

The crowd was chanting again. Trudy was gassed up on Diet Coke and Noel and ready for the spotlight once again. "Just a sec," she said. She pecked Noel on the cheek, then sprang from her stool. The crowd parted once again, cheering as she strutted to the stage.

Cassie stepped to the side of the mic, waiting for instructions. Trudy could tell she was tired. Dark circles underneath her eyes were starting to show through her make-up. She looked forlorn, waifish. Trudy hugged her there, onstage. "You were great," she said. "Just one more song, okay?"

As Cassie went to pick up her guitar, Trudy grabbed the mic. "Do you know what I just heard?" she croaked.

"What?" The audience replied as one.

"Noel wants me to join Ligeia. He asked me to be the new bass player."

There was some scattered applause. Harumi and Cassie watched her, their faces stricken with disbelief.

"But what about the Divas?" a young woman shouted from the front row.

"That's just it. I would never leave this band. These girls are my blood. Hell, we've even got a fan club." Now the applause was deafening. The whistles and shouts made Trudy's head pound. It was time for a song, but they'd already gone through their repertoire. They'd have to do a repeat. "Let's do 'Crashbaby' again," she said over her shoulder. "Cassie, you sing this time."

And then they were jamming again, using their last reserves of strength. The crowd, too, was on its second wind. It was the best party Trudy had ever been to, and there was no way she was going to break up Screaming Divas.

32

"Listen, love," Rebecca said, squeezing Esther's shoulder. "I've got a great idea."

Esther's muscles tightened. "What?"

"I think you should move in here with me after you graduate." Rebecca leaned down and brushed her cheek against Esther's. "What do you say?"

Rebecca's hand was sliding along her collarbone toward her breast. Esther was sure she could feel the wild reaction of her heart. She pressed her own hand over Rebecca's, halting its movement. "Um, I'll have to think about it."

In all honesty, she'd been having fantasies about getting an apartment with Harumi. Or Cassie. Or maybe even the whole band. Of course, her parents expected her to stay in a dorm next year. But Rebecca didn't show up in any of her daydreams.

Rebecca pulled away. She stalked across the room to the liquor cabinet and poured herself a drink. "Think about what?"

Esther's mouth was suddenly dry. She wet her lips. "Money, for one thing. It's not like you're paying me a living wage." She forced a laugh to show that she was teasing.

Rebecca took a swig of whiskey. "Did I say that I would make you pay rent?"

So she would be what? A kept woman? Rebecca already had control over most of her life. She chose Esther's clothes and told her how to wear makeup. She'd given her a job in her gallery. She'd gotten her into the Screaming Divas. Without Rebecca, Esther would be just another frumpy, slightly overweight wallflower, spending her weekends on the sofa with a box of Twinkies. Then again, sometimes that's exactly what she wanted to be.

This whole life she'd been living was beginning to feel more and more like a fraud. Sure, she had an authentic interest in paintings, and she'd learn to tell the difference between modernism and post-modernism and on a good day she could hold her own on the drums, but somewhere along the way she'd left her real self behind. Nobody knew her. Her parents had no idea that she was gay, and Harumi acted as if their mutual history were entirely forgotten. Rebecca thought that she knew Esther, but she was so absorbed in her Svengali role that she only saw what she wanted Esther to be, not who she really was. Esther wouldn't be able to withstand the pressure of having to be chic twenty-four hours a day.

"I think you'd get sick of me," she mumbled now.

"Sick of you?" Rebecca set down her drink and crossed the room to kneel at Esther's feet. "You silly goose," she said, smoothing back a strand of hair. "I love you. I'd never get sick of you."

Esther didn't respond. She didn't know how to begin to talk about her feelings. It was already too late. She'd been pretending all this time that everything was wonderful, that her old self was a loathsome stranger.

"And another thing," Rebecca said, moving away again. "I'd like you to tell your parents about us."

Tell them what, exactly? Once in a while she let Rebecca kiss her, but she wasn't ready to take things to the next level. So far, Rebecca had been understanding. Was this a sign that her patience was running out?

At any rate, she wasn't about to tell her mom and dad that she was gay.

"Darling, you're living a lie," Rebecca went on. "And so are your parents. You must tell them at some point."

Rebecca was right. Eventually, Esther needed to have a talk with her family. Otherwise, the lies would separate them forever. But there was so much else going on in her life at the moment that she couldn't deal with one more crisis. She'd have to come out in her own time.

"Rebecca, I'm sorry, but I need to take everything slowly," she said. "Please don't push."

Rebecca wrapped her arms around her midsection as if she were suddenly chilled. "Sometimes I'm afraid that I'm going to lose you," she said. Her voice was strangely hollow.

"No, never," Esther said, but even as the words left her mouth, she knew that she was lying.

There was no way Esther could tell Rebecca what she'd done. It had been totally spontaneous, almost an accident; if she'd given it any thought at all, she wouldn't have had the guts to invite Cassie home for Christmas.

The divas had been jamming in Trudy's living room a week before Christmas. Just for fun, they were singing "Jingle Bells" and "Rudolph, the Red-Nosed Reindeer," and other songs that they would never perform in public.

"So do we get a Christmas vacation?" Cassie had asked when they paused for a break. "Or do you expect us here on a holiday?"

"Why?" Trudy asked. "Do you have big plans?"

Cassie shrugged. "Not really. My dad's taking Johnette on a cruise and leaving me to fend for myself."

And that's when Esther had said, "You can come to our house. My mom loves having lots of people around at Christmas." It had just come out, like a sneeze.

Everyone in the room had looked at her strangely. Everyone, that is, except for Cassie, who'd smiled and said, "Sure, I'd love to." And then Trudy and Harumi had stared at Cassie. She and Esther rarely spoke during band practice and it wasn't as if they were buddies or anything. And they probably wondered about Rebecca.

Rebecca's idea for Christmas had been a cabin in the mountains, maybe a little bed and breakfast, but Esther had explained that her family would never forgive her if she went away. And then, of course, she had pushed for an invitation. "I'll bring English Christmas pudding. Your parents will love me."

Somehow, Esther wasn't so sure her mother and father would know what to do with her. Rebecca would strike them as some rare bird that needed special feeding. They'd be intimidated by her clothes and hair and accent. It would be too awkward.

"We'll go out the day after Christmas," Esther had promised. "I'll even treat you."

When she told her mother that Cassie was coming, Mrs. Shealy was thrilled. "I'm so glad you're making new friends," she said. "And how awful that Cassie's father would go off and leave her alone at Christmas, of all times!"

Esther's mother knew a little about Cassie's father. He was a prominent member of the community and, with his conspicuously young wife, a source of over-the-fence gossip. She even remembered the car crash that had taken Cassie's mother's life.

"You know, she was a looker. She was runner up to Miss South Carolina years ago. I saw her on TV." Esther's mother clucked. "But then she got started up with drinking. Some people said she was suicidal, said she couldn't stand losing her looks."

On Christmas Eve, Mrs. Shealy welcomed Cassie at the door with a hug.

"We're so glad you could join us," she cooed. She helped Cassie out of her pea coat and threw her hands up in surprise when Cassie handed her a package.

"A little something for under your tree," Cassie said.

Mrs. Shealy took the brightly wrapped parcel with one hand and guided Cassie deeper into the house with the other. "We've got a crowd here—Esther's grandparents and my sister and her family. I hope you won't mind sleeping with Esther."

How could she say such a thing! Esther's face turned crimson. "I'll sleep on the floor," she said quickly. "I have a sleeping bag."

"You promised to lend your sleeping bag to Cousin Bobby," Esther's mom said.

The turkey was already in the roaster and the house was starting to smell like a holiday dinner. Logs crackled in the fireplace. Esther trailed behind as Cassie took it all in—the stockings, Bing Crosby on the stereo, glass plates of fudge and peanut brittle.

Esther introduced Cassie to her relatives. She didn't tell her grandparents that they were in a punk rock band together. Esther noticed that they were all careful not to ask about Cassie's family.

Later that night, when everyone started trundling off to bed, Esther felt a rising panic. She wanted to stay up and watch TV in the living room, but one of her cousins was going to be sleeping on the sofa. They had no choice but to go to her room.

Esther sat down in the wicker chair in the corner. Cassie threw herself across the double bed.

"This must be kind of boring for you. Playing Monopoly with my cousins and everything . . . ."

"No, not at all," Cassie said. "It's better than being around my relatives. They all drink too much and start talking about Mama. It's horrid."

They were silent for a moment, the ghost of Cassie's mom hovering between them. Esther wasn't sure if she should say something about the accident or not. "What do you think Trudy's doing today?" she asked instead. She wondered why Cassie hadn't opted to spend the holiday with the lead diva. The two seemed so close.

Cassie grimaced. "Probably stalking Noel." And then, a couple of beats later, she asked, "So what's the deal with you and Rebecca?"

Esther froze. "What do you mean? Did Harumi say something?"

Cassie looked confused. "What? Harumi? No, I just wondered. I mean, obviously there's something going on between you two."

Esther could feel her face fill with warmth. Was it really so obvious? Did she have no secrets?

"It's no big deal," Cassie said, with a shrug. "If you don't want to talk about it, fine." She turned away and started thumbing through the record albums lined up on the bottom shelf of Esther's bookcase.

Esther took a deep breath. Cassie was her friend now. They were supposed to trust each other, to share secrets. "Yeah," she said, her voice breaking a little. "I guess we're involved. How could you tell?"

Cassie turned to face her, and hugged her knees. "Well, there's the way she looks at you, like she's ready to devour you. And the way you look at her, like you're nervous or scared or something."

Esther said nothing. She was ashamed of her fear, but she couldn't say why.

"So how do you feel about her?"

How *did* she feel? "Well, she's gorgeous, obviously. And smart, and she has that great London accent." Esther paused. "I wonder what she sees in me? She could have anybody."

"Maybe you're her type," Cassie said. "But you haven't really answered my question. Do you love her?"

Love? Esther tried to conjure a moment when she'd felt something like love. She admired Rebecca, yes. She was flattered by her attention. She'd even liked kissing her, but love? "I feel like I should love her," Esther said, finally. "I don't have a lot of people to choose from. Because I'm not, well, attracted to boys. So maybe this is my only chance to have someone. A partner."

Cassie rolled her eyes. "Do you really believe that? You shouldn't be with her unless you really care about her. It's not fair to either of you. And believe me, there are other people out there for you."

Everything that Cassie said made sense, but she didn't want to think about that right now. Maybe they could talk about Cassie's love life. It was her turn to spill.

"So what about you?" she asked.

"What *about* me?"

"There were rumors going around about you at school. You and Todd Elsworth." She didn't mention all the others—half the football team, plus one or two of the younger, better-looking male teachers, like Mr. Simpson, who taught science.

"We never even kissed."

The surprise must have shown on Esther's face. Her reaction quickly changed to embarrassment. Why had she believed all that talk, anyway? Cassie and two guys at once in the janitor's closet. Cassie with the class dopehead under the bleachers. Cassie, flashing the boys in Special Ed, just to get them worked up.

"I've never hooked up with anyone from school," Cassie said, "but I'm not a virgin. In case you were wondering."

Esther considered asking about Adam, but she didn't really want to hear about him. She would enjoy this night, having Cassie all to herself. It would probably never happen again.

"If you want, we can stay up for a while. Listen to music, or something."

"Actually, I'm pretty tired. Why don't we just turn in?"

Esther nodded. She got up and reached under her pillow for her yellow flannel pajamas. She turned away to lower her jeans and pull off her sweater. She wondered if Cassie was watching, but she didn't dare look behind her. When she had changed, she turned to find Cassie already snuggled beneath the covers. Her eyes were closed. Taking a deep breath, Esther climbed in beside her. She was careful not to touch Cassie, but she could feel the heat of her body under the blankets.

"Good night," she whispered.

"G'night."

Esther lay rigid, her heart battering her rib cage. There was no way she would be able to sleep. This was what she had dreamed about for years, but the dream come true was terrifying. Maybe it would be better to grab a blanket and make a nest in the hallway, she thought, but she didn't move. She lay there listening to Cassie's breathing, listening until it became deep and even. Then she rolled slowly onto her side.

There was just enough moonlight coming through the slit in the curtains for Esther to make out Cassie's face. Her golden hair was splayed on the pillow. The ironic set of her mouth had softened into an angel's kiss. In the dark, her scar was invisible.

Esther held her breath and reached a hand toward Cassie's pillow. With one finger, she stroked a lock of hair. It was soft as corn silk.

Suddenly, Cassie's eyes popped open and she laughed.

Esther drew back her hand.

"You thought I was asleep, didn't you?"

Esther buried her face in her own pillow. "I'm sorry. Your hair looked so soft. Not like mine, all wiry and wild."

Esther felt a hand on the back of her neck. Cassie's fingers worked their way up her nape, into the thick tangle of curls. "I'd love to have hair like this," she said.

Then Cassie was moving on top of her, and Esther felt her breath on the back of her neck, then lips. "If you want me to stop, just say so," Cassie whispered.

Esther felt fever spreading through her body. She wanted to roll over and touch Cassie, but she didn't dare. She held herself still as Cassie's fingers sneaked up her pajama top and traveled her bare back. She stayed on her stomach until Cassie moved off of her and nudged her onto her back.

When Cassie straddled her, Esther saw that she was naked. Her skin was glowing in the moonlight. As Cassie leaned down and began unbuttoning her top, Esther rose to kiss her.

33

Trudy was riding a city bus, trying not to inhale. The passenger next to her smelled of sweat and garlic. Someone had let out a fart.

She was trying not to listen, either. She was doing her best to tune out the endless nattering of the woman behind her. It wasn't that hard. Trudy had a radio in her head, and whenever she wanted, she could turn up the volume. Right now, Diana Ross and the Supremes were singing about living in shame and missing Mama. It was one of their older songs, recorded after Flo was gone and just before Diana set out on her own. Before things started to go downhill.

She was a little scornful of Diana for deserting the group. She'd never do that to her girls. And they'd never be Trudy Sin and the Screaming Divas. It sounded stupid, anyway.

She fingered the stuffing coming out of the ripped vinyl seat in front of her, then turned her attention to the scenery outside. They were passing through a neighborhood of one-story brick houses with neat lawns, many adorned with garlands of colored lights or pine branches.

Sometimes, when she found herself alone, she'd go out walking around. As she passed each house, she'd make up a little story about the people who lived there. She could sometimes see them through the windows, especially at night when the houses were lit up and she was covered by the dark. They'd be watching TV, or having dinner, or reading the newspaper.

Once she saw a mother and daughter dancing together. A waltz, it looked like. Maybe the woman was trying to teach her something. Trudy stood on the sidewalk watching until they missed a step and collapsed against each other in a fit of giggles. She and Sarah had never laughed like that together.

If only her mother had been a stay-at-home brownie baker—and she wasn't thinking of Amsterdam hash brownies—a one-man woman, someone who cared about what other people thought, even.

Instead, Trudy had gotten a mother who squeezed out babies and then played favorites. She wasn't really into the kids. She'd had her own agenda from day one. She'd wanted to rebel against her staid upbringing, the all-girls school, the white gloves and embossed stationery, "sir" and "ma'am." Trudy thought that she understood.

The bus wheezed to a halt and Trudy got off. She walked a couple of blocks under oaks and maples until she reached her destination. She stood at the foot of the driveway, unable to move any further, staring at her mother's house. It had been her house once, too, back before she'd gotten arrested.

She tried to guess at what was going on inside. Maybe Sarah was walloping Baby Ken, Trudy's latest baby brother, who must already be about two. Or maybe she was sitting on a pillow, meditating, trying not to think about all the sorry details of her life.

Sarah must have had big dreams at one time, something more than a series of loser husbands and this house in suburbia, but Trudy couldn't remember what they'd been.

She reached into her jeans pocket and felt the cassette—a tape of Supremes songs as covered by Screaming Divas. It wasn't studio quality; they didn't have that kind of money yet. But it would show Sarah that she'd been doing something with her life. That she was going to be somebody.

She took a deep breath and a step up the driveway. Then another, and another, till finally she was on the porch, at the door with her fingertip hovering over the glowing button of a doorbell.

What if Sarah wouldn't let her in the house?

She closed her eyes and summoned up whistles and applause, the girls in the front row who copied her clothes. She was a Diva, damn it, and nothing was going to get her down.

She pressed the doorbell.

She could hear the commotion inside—the blare of a TV, Ken's squalls, her mother's sharp voice. And then footsteps, a pause as someone looked through the peephole, followed by the jangle and clink of the chain lock. The door opened.

Sarah stood there, eyes narrowed, hip cocked, cigarette held like a roach. She took a drag, studied her daughter. "You'd better not be in some kind of trouble again."

Trudy ignored her and held out the cassette. Now seemed as good a time as any to give it to her. "Merry Christmas," she said. "I made this for you."

Ash from Sarah's cigarette dropped to the floor, but she didn't seem to notice. She put the butt in her mouth and squinted through the smoke as she examined the tape, turning it over and over in her hands.

Sarah looked older. It had been less than a year since they'd last met, but the crinkles that rayed out from her eyes were deeper. Her hair looked a little ratty and her roots were showing. Trudy wondered how her latest marriage was going, but she wasn't about to ask. She was still standing on the porch.

"I have a band now," she said. "We play in Columbia all the time. People say we're really good." She wished she'd brought them along for moral support. She tried to summon them now—Cassie, the golden one; Harumi, with her quiet strength; Esther, so full of goodness.

Sarah looked up then. "You look like you've lost some weight. Are you eating all right?"

"Yeah, Ma. And working hard. With my band."

"Huh. Your daddy was in a band once. He never made any money at it, though. Never got famous."

"I know. I lived with him for a while."

"Guess I knew that."

At last, Sarah opened the door wider and stepped back. It seemed that she'd figured out that Trudy wasn't about to torch the place.

"Well, let's see what this sounds like," she said, brandishing the tape.

The living room looked the same as she remembered—thick beige carpet, stained in some places from coffee spills, a maroon vinyl sofa, a glass-topped coffee table stacked high with magazines. An artificial Christmas tree hung with candy canes took up one corner. It was so utterly middle American that Trudy could hardly believe they'd ever lived in a teepee.

Just then, Ken toddled into the room. When he saw Trudy, he went for cover behind Sarah. He didn't remember her at all. Trudy guessed that her name never came up in conversation and that they didn't keep pictures of her around.

Her other half-brother and sister and Joey, her brother, were nowhere in sight. They were probably with their fathers for the holidays, as usual.

She plopped down on the sofa while Sarah tried to disentangle herself from the curly-haired boy attached to her legs.

"What's this?" she asked, nodding in the direction of the tape player. "Sounds like 'Baby Love.'"

Trudy's voice blasted out of the speaker, fast and frantic. You could hear her gulping for breath between phrases.

"Yeah, it is," she said. "We do a lot of Supremes covers."

Sarah shook her head. "You ruined my favorite song." But she was smiling. Amused. "You want something to drink? Beer? Iced tea?"

"Tea is okay."

Sarah kept talking as she went into the adjacent kitchen, Ken still tugging on her leg. "Ken, why don't you go say 'hey' to your sister?" And then, "So you're keeping out of trouble, huh? That's good. I heard Grandma and Grandpa were sending you some money and you know that if they hear anything bad, they'll cut you off. Like they did me."

"I know that."

Sarah came back with a tray of drinks and pretzels in a bowl. "You'd better eat a little. You look skinny."

They sat there, side by side, for a few minutes, listening to the tape.

"I guess now is as good a time as any to tell you that we'll be moving soon," Sarah said at last.

It figures, Trudy thought. She probably would have skipped town without saying a word if Trudy hadn't dropped in. Trudy stared at the ice in her drink.

"We're going to California," Sarah continued. "End of next month."

Well, California might be a cool place to visit someday. Trudy had always wanted to go to Hollywood. If things kept going well, maybe the Divas could go on tour out West.

"Good luck," she said, forcing herself to meet her mother's eyes.

Sarah reached out then as if she was going to touch Trudy's cheek or smooth down a strand of hair, but midway her hand dropped to the sofa. "I'm sorry," she said. "I know I haven't been the kind of mother you wanted."

Trudy shrugged. "I guess you did your best."

As soon as she finished her tea, she stood up. "I've got a bus to catch. See you later." She was walking out the door before Sarah had a chance to stop her. Or not. Her heart was banging like Esther's drums.

She was halfway down the driveway when she heard Sarah call out, "Thanks for the tape!"

"Hey, no problem," she shouted back. "Send me a postcard when you get where you're going."

34

On New Year's Eve, all of the Divas had been invited over to Cassie's house to watch Dick Clark. Her dad and step-mom were still off on their cruise. They wouldn't be back for another five days.

Cassie had invited Rebecca, too, but she had plans to go to some artist's party where there'd be a cash bar and a live band. Esther was relieved. She was also a little nervous. She hadn't seen Cassie since Christmas, although they'd talked on the phone a few times. Whenever she thought about that night, she felt uneasy. She remembered how her skin had tingled, how she had felt herself open to Cassie's fingers, but she also remembered how lonely she'd felt. When she'd looked up at Cassie, she'd seemed to be studying Esther like a science experiment. There had been no tenderness in those eyes. And then, when Esther had touched her back, she'd started moaning and wailing so loudly that her mother had come and tapped on the door to see if everything was all right. Mortified, Esther had tried to draw away, but Cassie had clamped her wrist between her thighs. It was almost as if she'd wanted Esther's mother to walk in.

Something had changed in Esther after that night. Instead of being in awe of Cassie, she now felt wary. And while the things they'd done together had made her feel good, she also felt violated, somehow. That wasn't love.

Esther changed from the sweat suit she'd been wearing all day into a pair of jeans and a pink mohair sweater she'd gotten for Christmas. She went into the kitchen, grabbed a couple of packets of microwave popcorn and her keys.

"Mom, I'm going now," she called out.

Her mother appeared in the doorway. "Esther, honey," she said, reaching over to pull a strand of hair out of her daughter's eyes, "I know there might be some drinking, and, well, if you need someone to drive you home, give us a call."

"Yes, Mom." She leaned forward and kissed her mother on the cheek.

Esther had never been to Cassie's house before, though she knew of the neighborhood. She'd jotted down directions on the back of an envelope as Cassie dictated them over the phone. Now she held the scrap of paper against the steering wheel as she drove. Left on Elm Street, right at the stop sign, four houses down. She found the big brick house without too much trouble. The sconces on the front porch were lit and a couple of cars were in the driveway. She recognized the Beetle as Cassie's.

She parked her car at the edge of the lawn so that she wouldn't get blocked in. She wanted to be able to leave whenever she felt like it. Then she trudged up the yard to the front door.

Cassie appeared almost as soon as she'd rung the bell. Her hair looked kind of stringy, and there were dark circles under her eyes. Esther wondered if she'd been sick. "Come in!" She reached for Esther's arm and pulled her inside. Trudy and Harumi were sitting on the floor, flipping through Cassie's record collection. Adam was there, too. Before, she would have been annoyed to find him there. He wasn't a Diva, after all, but tonight she felt relieved. If Adam and Cassie were together, Cassie wouldn't expect anything from her.

Esther took a look around. The room was tastefully furnished, with lots of cream jacquard. On the wall, there was an oil portrait of Johnette, Cassie's stepmother. Framed photos of Cassie and her father and stepmother were gathered on a shelf, but there was no sign of her real mother.

"Oops," Trudy said, knocking over a long-necked bottle. Everyone watched for a moment as the beer soaked into the plush, beige carpet.

"Fuck," Cassie said, after a few beats. She didn't seem mad, though. She picked up the bottle and disappeared for a moment. She came back with a roll of paper towels to sop up the mess.

Now the whole room seemed to stink of beer. There was also the fug of cigarette smoke and something else—that smell that sometimes lifted off Esther's brother's sheets when she did the laundry. It was Adam's smell, Esther realized. He and Cassie must have had sex before the others arrived.

Once again, Esther was surprised by how little she cared, how relieved she, in fact, felt. She wasn't ready for all that. She knew that now.

"What do you want to drink, Esther?" Harumi asked. "There's more beer. There're some wine coolers . . . ."

"I'll just have a Diet Coke," Esther said, remembering what her mother had said. "I don't feel that great." She was already thinking that she'd take off at midnight. She'd wait until the ball dropped at Times Square.

She followed Cassie into the kitchen, suddenly unsure of what to do with her hands.

"Umm, about Christmas Eve . . . ."

"Hey," Cassie said, handing her a cold can. "We'll always be friends, okay?"

Esther smiled. "Yes. Friends."

Back in the living room, Trudy flicked on the television. Dick Clark's face came into view. He was just announcing the first band, a bunch of blondes in miniskirts.

"Someday, we're going to be on the show," Trudy said.

The other Divas just stared at the TV screen, but Adam raised a cup into the air. "I'll drink to that."

"Wait," Cassie said. "I have something that we can truly celebrate." She disappeared in the back of the house.

Something about her and Adam? That painting of Cassie he'd been working on? Esther, Harumi, and Trudy exchanged glances. None of them seemed to know about the big surprise.

Cassie returned, hands behind her back. "Are you ready?"

"Enough with the suspense," Trudy growled, though even Esther could tell that she was enjoying this.

"Ta-da!" Cassie held out a piece of paper. A check. They all moved in for a closer look.

"My dad booked a studio so that we can record a demo, and this is going to cover the cost. It's his Christmas present to me. To all of us!"

It wasn't midnight yet, but they all started tearing paper napkins into paper confetti and kissing each other.

35

"So how are things going with Mr. Right?" Cassie asked Harumi.

It was post-gig—a private party at some sorority house, but a paid gig all the same—and the Divas were all gathered at the Capitol Café. Playing onstage made them ravenous.

"Do you mean Chip?" Harumi asked, perplexed.

"Who else, silly?" Cassie ruffled her hair.

"Not so well." She stirred the grits on her plate with a fork.

"Didn't I see him at The Cave last time we played there?" Trudy asked.

"Yeah, he was there," Harumi said. "I should have introduced you."

Actually, she hadn't even spoken to him that night herself. Of course she'd seen him. He'd dressed down in jeans and a polo shirt, but he still looked out of place. She could imagine his discomfort, and it had moved her that he would go out of his way to prove his interest. He risked blasted eardrums and stomped-on Topsiders, all for her. Their eyes had met briefly before a taller man stepped in front of him. Then the house lights had dimmed and the overhead lights brightened, and Harumi couldn't see faces anymore.

Playing back that night in her mind, she thought she should have had a song dedicated to him, or thrown her pick, or committed some other showy rock star gesture. She should have talked to him, at least, but she was still too embarrassed and too tired. Maybe it was better to retreat from the real world for a while. She could deal with Mrs. Harris and her paperback novels and scratchy old records. That was just one woman's nostalgia. And she could lose herself in the music, in the intricate movements of her fingers, whenever she was with the Divas. Even at Goatfeathers she could disappear into a role, as long as Chip didn't show up. (And he didn't; he was giving her space.) She liked to daydream about him, but she wasn't ready to deal with a flesh and blood man.

"So what's the problem?" Trudy asked. "Was The Cave too spooky for him?"

Harumi shrugged. "He sent me flowers every day for a week after that." The notes were always short—the first one, an apology, and then a note to "The Rickenbacker Goddess," praising her performances. She'd arranged the flowers by her bed so she could wake to the sight of roses and hothouse orchids. The notes, she'd saved in the pages of her favorite books.

"Wow. What a romantic! I can't imagine Adam sending me flowers," Cassie said.

Trudy snorted.

"No one has ever sent me flowers, either," Esther added.

Harumi knew she'd never had a boyfriend. Maybe girls didn't send flowers to each other.

Sooner or later Chip would give up on her, if he hadn't already. The last note had included his phone number and the words "call me." If she ignored it, he'd fade from her life and find someone else.

"Do you like him?" Cassie asked.

"Yeah. I do. I just don't know how to behave. Last time we were together, he was kissing me, when I thought of something funny and I started laughing." She raked through her grits again with the fork. "It wasn't even that funny. I was just nervous."

"Harumi." Cassie waited until she looked up from her plate. "He doesn't care. He came to our show just to see you, and he sent you flowers. You should call him."

"Call him right now," Trudy said. She jerked her head toward the pay phone in the corner. It was after midnight.

"No way."

"Call him! Call him!" Trudy started chanting. And then Esther and Cassie joined in, until they were loud enough to attract the attention of everyone in the restaurant. Even Pee Wee, the waitress.

She sashayed over with a pot of freshly brewed coffee and filled their cups. "Girl, you need to get on that phone."

She pushed her plate away and swung her body out of the booth.

"Here's a quarter," Cassie said, holding out a coin.

Harumi took it. Slipped it in the slot. Punched in the number. She'd memorized it by now. She thought about hanging up after the second or third ring, and again after Chip's first "Hello."

"Who's this? Is anyone there?"

When she sensed he was about to slam the receiver down in agitation, she spoke. "Wait, Chip. It's me."

She heard him sigh and imagined the tension leaving his shoulders, his body relaxing to the tune of her voice. Maybe he was smiling.

"Harumi." He recognized her voice even though they'd never spoken on the phone before. "How are you?"

She took a deep breath, not knowing what she really wanted to say. "I'm sorry. I wasn't laughing at you."

"I know. Do you want to give us another try?"

"Okay."

"How about Saturday night?"

When she hung up the phone, Cassie and Esther and Trudy made her repeat every word. Pee Wee brought her a piece of pecan pie and told her it was on the house.

When Chip showed up at six-thirty on Saturday night, he was wearing a tux with a white scarf tossed around his neck. Fancy. He hadn't told her where they were going, but obviously she was underdressed. He waited for Harumi to change out of her leotard and wrap skirt and into a black dress. Then he ushered her out to his car.

"Tonight, we're going to listen to my kind of music," he said, starting the engine.

Harumi's stomach flip-flopped. She hoped he was taking her to some quiet bar with a singer-songwriter on a stool, or even a disco where thirtysomething couples shagged to beach music. She didn't want to be reminded of her previous life.

A few minutes later, they pulled up in front of the Township auditorium and Harumi saw the marquee: Carolina Symphony with Anne-Marie Muller. Classical music. Violin soloist.

Harumi didn't say a word as Chip parked the car and opened her door. She let her small hand rest lightly on his elbow as they walked to the entrance. Women with stiffly styled hair and long gowns swished through the lobby.

Harumi had heard of Anne-Marie. She was one of the most famous young violinists in the world: a child prodigy, a daring original who sometimes stomped onstage in black leather. Once she'd shocked an audience by appearing in blue jeans, but she'd been quickly forgiven when she put bow to strings.

Chip had secured good seats, only twenty rows from the stage. They'd be close enough to watch Anne-Marie's face—the expressions of effort and genius.

Harumi sat rigidly, her back not even touching the velvet-upholstered seat. She could feel Chip's eyes upon her. Maybe he thought she wasn't used to such a luxe environment.

She felt his hand hovering above her own, and she took it and held it on her lap. Why was she so nervous? She wasn't even the one performing. She took a deep breath and eased back into her seat.

"Are you okay?" Chip asked. "You look a little pale."

Harumi gave him a small smile and squeezed his hand lightly.

Finally, the stage cleared and the house lights dimmed. The audience applauded as the orchestra took their places. The applause increased when the conductor appeared. And then Anne-Marie, resplendent in an iridescent pink strapless gown, stepped from behind the curtain. Her hair spouted from a high ponytail and spilled into her face. She looked gorgeous. A front row fan whistled.

When the music began, Harumi closed her eyes. She could see, even then, the bows slicing air, the dance of the conductor's baton.

She could feel her own calloused fingers pressing against strings. She could smell the piney resin.

They were playing Vivaldi's *Four Seasons* concerti, and when Anne-Marie took up the sweet, joyous notes of the Spring concerto her face was filled with something akin to love. Harumi knew that she had lost that look in her last year of playing the violin. Her passion had turned into resentment. She had been right to quit. Still, listening now, she wondered what it would be like to lift an instrument—Sadie III?—to her shoulder.

Her eyes stayed open from then on, fixed on the performers. Nothing distracted her, not even the snoring of the man next to her. She almost forgot about Chip as well. At intermission, she turned to him at last.

"Your cheeks are blooming," he said. "You look like an angel."

"She's brilliant, isn't she?" Harumi nodded to the place where Anne-Marie had stood, tossing her ponytail.

"She made a deal with the devil, that one," Chip said with a wink. "Care for a cup of coffee?"

They went into the lobby, into the hum and buzz of ordinary conversation, and had espresso.

"I've missed you," Chip said.

"Me, too." Looking up at him now, she couldn't believe she'd been so silly and nervous. She felt completely at ease.

He leaned close to brush a stray hair from her cheek and she inhaled his musk. She felt a flash of desire and wondered, for a moment, if she would make love to him that night. But no. It was too soon. She would have to tell him that.

The lobby lights clicked off and on and they returned to their seats.

"Chip," she whispered, just before the orchestra reappeared. "I have something to tell you."

"What?"

Harumi took a deep breath. "I've never had a boyfriend before, and I play the violin."

36

It was a week before Valentine's Day, and it was snowing. Esther hugged her body as she ran from Trudy's door to her car, her teeth chattering. No matter how cold it was, though, she was glad to be out of Trudy's living room. The lead Diva had been in one of her moods. She'd actually flung a beer bottle against the wall, putting a dent in the plaster, when Cassie messed up on a chord progression. Not a good scene.

And Cassie, well, she'd been acting strange lately. Spacey. Sometimes she started laughing or crying for no reason. And she'd been losing weight and color. Esther was sure she was on some kind of drug.

Harumi was the only one who seemed normal. If anything, Harumi seemed happier than usual. She no longer sat in the corner, caressing her bass. Now she actually laughed at Trudy's off-color jokes. She was quicker to make suggestions on improving songs. And this evening, once or twice she'd exchanged looks with Esther, rolling her eyes when Trudy threw the bottle.

Esther waited till the car was warmed up, then stabbed a tape into her cassette deck. She warbled along as she made her way home.

She'd promised to call Rebecca later, but she had a biology test to study for and a paper to write. Plus, she wasn't in the mood. Rebecca would want to discuss Valentine's Day plans—sex on a public beach, or something equally outrageous—and Esther wasn't up for it. She was dreading the fourteenth of February. She wished they could just exchange boxes of chocolate and be done with it.

Rebecca. Lately, just the thought of her mentor/friend/boss gave Esther a headache. She knew that there was something very wrong with the relationship. It was time to put an end to it, but Esther didn't know how. If she had the money and the guts, she'd leave town without a forwarding address. That would be the easiest way.

Or she could write a letter. Breaking up by mail was cowardly, but she was a coward. She'd be the first to admit it. Besides, in a live, one-to-one confrontation, she'd either lose her courage or wind up being persuaded by Rebecca to change her mind. And then she'd continue being miserable. A letter would be best.

Esther reached the house just as the tape was ending. Her mother had left the porch light on, and Esther could see the snow whirling around. She sat in her car for a moment, letting her decision harden into something concrete. Then she took a deep breath and yanked the door handle.

Almost as soon as she was in the foyer, her mother rushed out to greet her.

"Oh, honey. We were worried about you. Were the roads icy?"

Esther kissed her cheek. "No, not at all."

"Your boss called a little while ago. She wants you to call her back."

Esther gritted her teeth and nodded. She wouldn't call. Instead, she ducked into the living room to say hello to her father, enthroned as usual in his La-Z-Boy with a cold beer, and hurried upstairs to her room.

As she lay sprawled across her bed, she tried to concentrate on "A Rose for Emily," but thoughts of Rebecca kept barging into her mind. She finally gave up, closed her book, and took out a notebook.

"*Dear Rebecca,*" she wrote, "*I am unhappy in our relationship and I don't want to be your girlfriend anymore.*"

With Rebecca, she knew, it was best to be direct.

She was going to have to give up her job, but that was okay. She'd socked away quite a bit of money over the past few months, and she was sure she could find something else. She'd sling burgers at McDonald's, if need be.

At one in the morning, after four drafts had already been crumpled and tossed, Esther finished her letter. She signed it, stuffed it into an envelope, and went downstairs to get a stamp out of the kitchen drawer. Then she slipped back out into the cold, hopped in her car, and drove to the nearest mailbox.

She wouldn't go to work tomorrow. She'd leave a note at the gallery and that would be it.

When she got back home, she went straight to bed. William Faulkner would have to wait.

She thought that relief would wash over her immediately, that sleep would come easily, but she tossed and turned all night. The letter in the mailbox was like a bomb waiting to go off. At dawn, after a few twisted dreams, she dragged herself out of bed and splashed her face with cold water. Her eyes in the mirror were red-rivered and shadowed.

All day long, she found herself looking over her shoulder, as if Rebecca might be there, ax in hand. It was silly. The letter hadn't even been delivered yet, but in her sleep-starved state, paranoia ruled.

By the time she got home that night, after classes and band practice, she was too tired to care. She glanced at the note her mother had left on the table—"Call Rebecca"—and shredded it. Then she dove into bed.

It was not until two days later, at four in the afternoon, that Rebecca showed up on the Shealy family's front porch.

Esther heard a car tear into the driveway, heard a door slam, and quick steps on the sidewalk. This was followed by the doorbell—three impatient rings. She crept to the window knowing what she'd find, and there it was—Rebecca's red Mustang.

She heard her mother chirping downstairs, and then Rebecca's deeper voice.

"Esther, honey? Could you come down here, please?" Her mother's voice was obscenely cheerful. She had no idea what was about to go down.

Wild thoughts caromed in her head. She could jump out the window and flee across the lawn, or hide herself under the bed. If she just ignored them . . . but now her mother was banging on the door. "Esther? You have a visitor." Damn that singsong voice. She'd be setting out coffee and home-baked cookies any minute now.

"Coming."

Rebecca stood in the foyer in a sharp tweed suit. She looked great, totally unaffected, and Esther wondered if she had gotten the letter.

"Hey," she said, not knowing what else to say.

"Hello."

They stared at each other for a moment, then Rebecca reached into her jacket pocket and pulled out the letter. "We need to talk."

Esther's mother bustled in the background, her ears, no doubt, alert. "Let's go someplace. We can sit on the porch." It was cold, but she didn't want Rebecca in her house.

To her relief, Rebecca followed her outside and took a seat beside her on the cement steps.

The first words she said were, "You have devastated me."

Esther hung her head. "I'm sorry."

"What happened? We were so happy. We loved each other." Her voice was getting louder, verging on the hysterical. Esther hoped her mother was minding her own business.

"Is there someone else? Some boy?"

Esther shook her head. It was true. She was cured of Cassie, after all this time.

"Don't you love me anymore?"

Esther could see that her hands were trembling. She was truly falling apart. Part of her wanted to soften the blow, but she knew what she had to do. "No," she said. "I never loved you. Not from the beginning."

And then Rebecca was wailing, clawing at Esther's face, and the door opened. Esther's mother stepped out onto the porch and bent down. "Is everything okay?"

"It will be," Esther said. She squeezed Rebecca's shoulder once, one final time, and disappeared into the house.

37

Cassie was late. Trudy would probably be furious, but she'd get over it. After all, she wasn't the one who'd booked the studio. And the money was coming from Cassie's daddy.

By some weird coincidence, he'd reserved studio time on the anniversary of her mama's death. They'd never done anything formal to recognize the day, so she assumed he wasn't aware of it. He'd probably forgotten. Or maybe it was his feeble attempt to distract her from grief. But this day always made her feel edgy and sad. She had a hard time concentrating.

When she screeched up to the curb, she saw them standing there on the sidewalk, Trudy, in jeans and a cracked leather jacket, shifting from foot to foot; Harumi, hugging her bass; and Esther, hovering nearby. Cassie knew that since Rebecca was no longer helping out, Esther wasn't sure of her place in the band. But she'd come along as a drummer. She was good at it, and she was dependable. All of them ought to praise her more.

"Hey, y'all," she shouted. "Sorry I'm late!"

Esther's face lit up with what looked like relief. "We thought you were . . . ." Her eyes darted from Trudy to Harumi, and back to Cassie again.

"What?"

"We thought you were shooting up with Adam," Trudy said, looking her straight in the eye.

They knew? How could they know? She'd been so discreet, keeping her arms covered, her mouth shut.

"Look," Trudy said. "This band means a lot to me. I don't want you to screw it up."

"It means a lot to me, too," she said, annoyed. It's not like she was some junkie, selling herself on street corners, desperate for her next fix. She had it under control. "We're worried about you," Harumi put in, quickly. "What you're doing is dangerous."

Sweet, innocent Harumi. Cassie spread her arms and gathered them in a group hug. "I'm totally fine. I just thought I'd give it a try, once or twice, for kicks. I'm not addicted. So don't you worry about me."

When they came out of their huddle, she could tell that Harumi and Esther were reassured, but Trudy—she'd need a little more convincing.

"Come on," she said, waving them on like a tour conductor. "We've got a demo to record!"

Once they were all set up in the studio, Cassie turned things over to Trudy. She wasn't interested in keeping everyone in line, anyway.

Trudy reached into her pocket and pulled out a piece of paper that had been folded into an origami crane. She flattened it and read aloud. "Okay, we're going to do 'Crashbaby' and 'Lady Lazarus Rises Again' first, just to make sure we get those tracks laid down. I think those are going to be our hits." This, with a nod to Cassie. "And then we'll do Esther's song."

"Really?" Esther's eyes flooded with tears.

"It's a good song," Harumi said, quietly.

Cassie nodded in agreement. Tell her now, she thought, willing Trudy to be nice. Tell her what she means to us.

"You've proven yourself to be a true Diva," Trudy said. "And this song has actually kind of grown on me. Plus, it's sometimes good to slow down once in a while, give ourselves a break."

They hadn't practiced it all that much, but Cassie was sure they'd be able to conjure some rough beauty.

The studio sound engineer was waiting for his cue on the other side of the glass. They put on their earphones, adjusted their mics, and did a sound check.

"Are you ready?" Trudy asked.

They all screamed at once, "Yes!"

By the end of their allotted time, they'd managed to record five songs. It was a solid sampler, enough to give local DJs and record companies a taste of their talent. As they were packing up, they made plans to celebrate at the Capitol Café.

"Before that, would you mind doing me a favor?" Cassie interrupted.

"Anything," Trudy said. "As long as it doesn't involve Adam."

A low blow, but Cassie figured she'd ignore it. "Would you all go with me to Mama's grave?"

"Of course we will," Esther said. It was as if now that her initiation was complete, she was free to speak up.

They all moved closer. She could feel their warmth, their strength. This must be what it's like to have sisters, she thought.

"What did your mama like?" Harumi asked.

"What did she like?" What a strange question.

Harumi shook her long hair out of her eyes as she tried to explain. "When we went to Japan, after my grandfather died, we laid his favorite things at the family altar. Like tangerines and green tea. To keep his ghost happy, I guess."

Cassie nodded. She was pretty sure the spirit of her mother wasn't happy. Whenever she dreamed about Mama, she was raging. "She liked to drink. And she was really, really into beauty pageants." She rolled her eyes, but Harumi just nodded thoughtfully.

"Okay, let's go," Trudy said.

They caravanned to the cemetery and parked in a row under some oak trees. Dusk was falling. The sky was edged in pink, and bats swooped over their heads as they walked across the lawn to her mother's grave. Talk about spooky.

Cassie walked up to the headstone and traced her mother's name—Leticia Anne Haywood—with her fingers. "Hi, Mama," she whispered. "I'm sorry I've been away so long."

Usually, on this day, she lit a candle in her room and talked to the ceiling, imagining that her mother was listening. Sometimes she cried a little. But she was always alone.

Harumi stepped forward and put her left hand on Cassie's back. In her right hand, she held a tube of lipstick, which she placed in front of the stone. Trudy came next, with a mini bottle of whiskey. And then Esther. "Did your mama like music?" she asked. "Maybe we could sing something for her."

Cassie's eyes were filling with tears. "She did," she said, with a little laugh, dragging her wrist across her nose. "She trained me to sing 'How Much Is That Doggie in the Window?' It was my stage number. She had it all choreographed. Do you know it?"

"Wait here," Harumi said. "I'll get my bass."

A few minutes later, after a quick lesson, they were all singing a raucous punk version together. Cassie thought that they sounded good, but her mama was probably turning over in her grave.

38

At the end of April, the Divas were in a rented van, plowing through the night. "Crashbaby" had started getting airplay on WUSC, the local college radio station. They'd be opening for Ligeia the next evening at a club in Washington, DC. This was the big time, baby. Trudy inhaled the scent of leather seats and closed her eyes. Soon they'd have their own van—no, a bus!—with "Screaming Divas" splashed on the side in DayGlo colors. Maybe they'd have the whole thing carpeted inside with bright pink shag.

Trudy was so caught up in her fantasy that she didn't notice Noel disappearing from the seat across the aisle. He'd been snoozing only minutes before, a thin line of drool hanging from his lip. She twisted around in her seat and saw him sitting next to Cassie. Their heads were bent close together, and they were giggling about something.

Trudy was too keyed up to sleep. She just sat there, listening to Alan's snores and Esther's lip-smacking and the hum of the van engine. There was nothing to look at outside. It was black, the moon behind clouds. Instead, she looked at the pictures in her head—the Divas on an arena stage, buff boys tossing up their boxer shorts, the crowd shrieking for more.

They pulled into a Maryland diner at dawn. The Divas piled into one booth, Ligeia into another. Across the table, Cassie seemed spacey. Distracted. Trudy wondered if she was on something. Then again, maybe she was just sleepy.

"Are you going to be all right tonight?" Trudy asked her.

"Sure."

"How about you, Esther?"

"Yeah. I mean, I think so." Her pale cheeks flooded with pink.

Trudy had been riding her hard, like some kind of dominatrix, but Esther had actually improved over the past month or so. Post-Rebecca, she'd started to relax a little more. She tossed her hair around when she was hitting the drums, and made those rock star grimaces you always saw on TV. Esther had become fun lately.

Trudy glanced over at Harumi, who was shoveling hash browns into her delicate mouth. She looked rested and serene. Trudy didn't have to worry about Harumi. She might have concerns about Harumi's dad showing up, but he wouldn't be driving all the way to DC to cause a scene.

They'd been so pumped up about this trip that they'd managed to write three new songs over the past two weeks. They'd practiced every day for three to five hours, then lounged around talking about what they'd wear. Trudy had a little go-go dress with tiers of fringe that she'd found at a vintage clothing store. She was going to wear it with white majorette boots. Very sixties. Harumi had decided on one of her Goatfeathers outfits—a simple black dress and fishnet hose. Esther, who didn't have Rebecca to dress her anymore, would probably wear what she always wore—one of those Indian print peasant dresses. And Cassie, well, she said she was saving it for a surprise.

A couple of hours later, they were stretching their limbs in front of the club, glad to be out of the van at last. Trudy scoped the premises with approval. The Kit Kat Club occupied an old warehouse by the Potomac River. The outside was weathered wood, deliberately spray-painted with graffiti. There was a big dirt lot for parking. Trudy didn't see a marquee, but the regulars probably knew what was going on anyhow. No doubt flyers were plastered all over town. She had faith that the buzz was out about Ligeia and Screaming Divas.

They were greeted by Leo, a cute young guy with dyed blond hair and a trio of hoops hooked through his left earlobe. "Hello," he said, almost bowing. "Welcome. We're glad you found your way here."

He invited them inside for a beer, then gave them the grand tour—the dressing room (which they'd have to share), bathroom, phone booth, the hall of fame. The latter was a dark corridor, walls signed on both sides by various visiting artists. "I'd be honored," Leo said, "if you'd all leave your mark."

Trudy had already decided that she was going to sign right next to Patti Smith's autograph.

After they'd unloaded their equipment with the help of a couple of Kit Kat employees, set up, and done a sound check, both bands ran through a couple of songs. By then it was time for dinner.

Leo took them to a Thai restaurant in downtown DC. "One of my friends saw your show down in Atlanta," Leo told Noel. "He said you were awesome."

"Wait'll you hear us," Trudy couldn't help interrupting. "Your ears will have orgasms."

Leo laughed and gave Trudy a long look. He was checking her out. Weighing his chances. Well, he could dream as long as he wanted, but she belonged to Noel. She flipped her hair back and lit a cigarette.

By the time they got back to the club, they were all a little buzzed on East Asian beer. It was just after dusk. The sky was purple and bruised. Cars had already started filling the parking lot.

Ligeia was going to play in their street clothes, so the Divas had the dressing room to themselves for a while. Trudy slipped away to check out the stage, then reported back. "There're already people camped out in front of the stage," she said. "Must be forty or fifty in the club right now."

Leo had predicted that the place would be jam-packed. The regulars turned out like clockwork on a Friday night. Plus, people had heard about Ligeia. Even this far up the coast, they were getting airplay on college radio.

Harumi was sitting on a stool against the cinderblock wall, thumbing through an old copy of *Melody Maker*. Esther, afloat in her ethnic dress, was ratting out her hair with a brush. And Cassie was half-naked, standing there in her black lace bra and panties, looking like some demented Victoria's Secret model. For a second Trudy wondered if she was planning on going out like that, but then she dipped down and pulled a dress out of her zip-top duffel bag. And what a dress it was. Trudy watched while she slithered into gold lamé. It was tight and dazzling and it would catch all the light. No one would be able to look at anything else.

Trudy felt a flicker of jealousy, but she quickly extinguished it. Sure, Cassie looked like a goddess, but what was good for her was good for the band. They were all in this together. Anyway, it wasn't about the clothes; it was about the music. Tonight they would be their most sensational selves. They'd ignite those Yankees with their fire.

Esther was sitting on a vinyl sofa against the wall, eyes closed, breathing in through her nose and exhaling through her mouth. Some kind of meditation thing. Trudy plopped down next to her.

A few minutes later, Ligeia streamed into the room, Leo close behind. "Whenever you're ready," he said. "Pick your moment."

Trudy patted the space between her and Esther, but Noel ignored her. "Nice dress," he said to Cassie.

"How's the crowd?" Trudy asked, meaning to bring the topic back to business. "Is it filling up?"

She'd directed the question to Noel, but Alan answered. "Respectable," he said. "Nothing like what we had in Atlanta, but not bad, really."

And then Alan's eyes were on Cassie, too, and he was moving to her side, trying to get her attention.

Gretchen, the new bass player, was seemingly oblivious. She yawned widely and looked around for a place to sit.

Trudy didn't know much about Gretchen. She was tall and slender and wore boys' clothes—jeans and T-shirts that were too small, rising above her bellybutton. Her hair was fine and limp and cut chin-length.

On the van, all the way from Columbia, Trudy had only heard her voice once or twice. Whenever she'd looked back, Gretchen had been reading or napping. The guys talked about her musical expertise, but Trudy knew that no one in that town could play better than Harumi.

The noise was louder now. Maybe there were more people, maybe they were just drunker, but the babble of voices was almost drowning out the piped-in music. The natives are getting restless, Trudy thought.

She got up from the sofa, planted her fists on her hips, and said, "Showtime, girls."

Esther's eyes popped open in panic. Harumi slid down from her stool and tossed the magazine she'd been reading on a low table. Cassie stretched cat-like toward the ceiling, then prowled toward the exit.

"Break a leg," Noel said, sinking into the now-vacant sofa.

Trudy bent and kissed him full on the mouth. "Y'all can eat our dust, baby."

He laughed.

The four Divas looked at each other in turn, then pushed through the door and followed the corridor to the stage.

As soon as they appeared, the audience started to amass around the platform, like ants to a crumb. They were focused, ready, and Screaming Divas would give them everything they hoped for. Trudy was sure of it.

As they were taking up their instruments, Leo came to the front mic. He waited for a cue, then announced, "Let's welcome tonight's opening band, all the way from Columbia, South Carolina: Screaming Divas!"

They opened with the dissonant chords of "Lady Lazarus Rises Again," and the sea of heads began to bob and bounce.

Trudy hurled herself into the song—"*This is number one! I did it with a gun!*"—flailing and jerking till sweat dripped from her hairline. Bodies writhed and danced. Fists punched the air. Hoots followed. And that was only the first number.

Trudy fed on the energy, becoming wilder and wilder as the set went on. She jumped, did cartwheels, even dove into the mosh pit and body-surfed from stranger to stranger.

She thought that they could keep playing forever, but then her voice started to rust. Her throat was raw by the time they reached the one hundred minute mark.

"Hey," she tossed over her shoulder. "Why don't we do Esther's song?" They'd only practiced it a few times, but this seemed like the perfect place to try it out. The crowd was theirs. They could do no wrong at this point. She handed the mic to Cassie. "Want to sing?"

Trudy stepped back and let Cassie into the spotlight.

"*Last night I had the craziest dream / you were waltzing in a moonbeam.*" Her voice trembled at first, shimmery like her dress.

The crowd became quiet, still, as if they were scared for her, waiting to catch her if she fell. But as the song progressed, her voice became louder and stronger, and the silence became like worship.

"*We share the same blood / We're sisters under the skin.*" As she belted out the chorus, Trudy had this strange desire to kiss her. She was magnificent.

At the end, Cassie drooped on the stage, as if she were so precious and rare, that she was only meant to sing that one song, and to sing it perfectly. Whistles and hoots came from the deepest recesses of the hall. And then—surprise, surprise—Noel jumped out onto the stage. He leaned in next to Trudy to help sing "Wicked Ways," one of their newer songs. Ligeia was ready to take over and Trudy was tired, so she gave in. After a final impromptu bass solo from

Harumi, and a repeat of the chorus, Trudy shouted, "Thank you." The Divas deserted the spotlight.

Backstage, still panting, Trudy hugged them all. Huddled in solidarity, they mingled girl sweat and shampoo scents. "We were jamming," she said. "We were the best we've ever been." She stood back and looked into their glowing faces. She could tell that adrenaline was gushing through their veins. "I'm proud of you. All of you."

There was a little tap on the door. Leo stuck his head in. "A smash success," he said. "Here. Compliments of the house." He brought in a cooler of beer and a plate of nachos, the cheese all gooey and warm.

Trudy grabbed a can of beer and held it over her head, letting the condensation dribble onto her upturned face. "I'm so happy," she said. She closed her eyes and rolled the can over her chest.

Then she heard the music start up—the deep thrum of Gretchen's bass, John's guitar, Noel's brooding voice. She could hear Alan bashing on the drums and the wail of the crowd as they recognized the band's first song from college radio. Even though she'd been ready to collapse on that cheap vinyl sofa a few seconds before, the music charged her up again. "I'm going to go out there and dance," she said. She waited a second and, when no one made a move to follow, pushed through the door and into the hall.

Trudy stood at the back long enough to down her beer, then began squirming through the throng. She shoved elbows and hips aside as she made her way to the front. A couple of people swore at her, but she didn't care. By the end of the second song, she was close enough to spit onto the stage. She could look right into Noel's eyes. If she reached out, she could catch drops of his sweat on her palm. There, so close to the speakers, she could feel Noel's voice reverberating on her bones.

As he sang, he wrapped his arms around his shoulders. He bent over, leaning heavily on his knees, singing with such pain that it made Trudy want to jump up there and comfort him. But then he looked up at the audience and his eyes were demonic. He hated them all. And his music had possessed them.

For a split second, she envied his crowd control. She had to work so hard, sweating her ass off, but he just stood there and they were his. The feeling passed quickly. He's going to be mine, she thought. All mine. And they were both going to be famous.

Trudy was as disappointed as the rest of them when the band left the stage for the final time. The lights came on overhead and suddenly the place was filled with ghouls. The makeup that had looked so cool in the dark—the slashes of rouge and thick black eyeliner—looked hideous in the light. Party's over, Trudy thought. It was way past midnight. They'd have a few beers with ol' Leo, then sleep all the way home in the van.

Trudy found Harumi and Esther on stools at the back. "Where's Cassie?" she asked.

A look passed between them.

Trudy raised her eyebrows, but no one said anything.

The club was clearing out quickly. Alan appeared, trailed by Gretchen. The two of them slumped down against the wall. Next John showed up, his shirt unbuttoned, revealing a line of fuzz. "We've got to make a tape soon," he said, cracking his knuckles. "We could make lots of money. These people loved us. We could have had them eating off of our butts."

"They loved us, too," Trudy said, cocking her hip. "Pretty soon you'll be opening for us."

John rolled his eyes. "Yeah, right."

Harumi yawned widely. "I think I'm going to crawl into the van and sleep," she said.

"Me, too." Esther slid off her stool.

"What's wrong with y'all? Don't you want to celebrate?"

"We did already," Harumi said. "Backstage. Where were you?"

How could they be such deadbeats? They were on the verge of big time success and all they wanted to do was snooze. This was a time for serious partying.

"Where's Leo?" she asked.

John shrugged. "I have no idea. But he better show up soon because we've got to get paid."

Trudy stormed off down the corridor. The dressing room door was locked. She rattled the knob, then pounded on the door. "Who's in there?"

Silence. And then there was a giggle. Cassie. Who was she in there with? Leo? He'd been seriously checking her out all evening. Well, good for her. She needed to get away from Adam, anyhow. "C'mon. Open up."

Trudy pressed her ear against the door. She could hear grunts and the squeak of vinyl. A rhythmic beat. Then a high-pitched scream. Cassie was screwing Leo. Trudy smirked and leaned against the opposite wall to wait.

A few minutes later, she heard footsteps, the slip of the bolt, and the door swung open. She froze.

"What?" Noel asked. He stood there in his jeans with the zipper open. Behind him, Cassie was sprawled nude over the sofa. She was still giggling.

Trudy felt as if some beast was tearing out her stomach. She could feel bile rising in the back of her throat and then the burn of tears. No, damn it. She wasn't going to cry. She bit her lip so hard she drew blood. Trudy Sin didn't cry. She was a warrior.

She flew at Noel first, clawing at his bare chest and face. Her fingernails ripped his cheek, trailing a ribbon of blood. Noel grabbed at her, trying to catch her wild hands, but she was too quick for him. She slithered out of his grasp and went for Cassie.

"How could you?" she yelled. "I thought you were my friend!" She grabbed a fistful of blonde hair and yanked. "You can walk home for all I care 'cause you're not riding back with me. You're out of my life."

She reached for Cassie's throat, but then Noel was behind her, latching his elbow around her neck.

"Knock it off," he said in her ear. "I never promised you anything, Trudy."

No, he hadn't, but Cassie had. Maybe not in words, but in spirit. Trudy had considered her a sister, a soulmate. Now she was just a traitor.

39

When all was said and done, Cassie wasn't sure why she had done it with Noel. It had been a whim, a good idea at the time.

On the way to DC, when he'd dropped into the seat beside her, she had been surprised. They'd never really talked before.

"You should try to sing more often," Noel whispered to her, his lips brushing her earlobes. "Just tell Trudy what you want. Stand up for your rights."

Cassie laughed. "Maybe I should just quit and form my own band."

Noel had looked at her for a moment in total seriousness. "Maybe you should."

She knew that he was serious about music, that he was planning on making Ligeia his whole life. He told her that he had dropped out of college after one semester. He'd been working at a print shop to make ends meet. He lived poorly, but he had enough money for new guitar strings. Maybe this recording that they were going to make would change things. Maybe he'd move to Atlanta, or even L.A.

Cassie didn't know exactly what she wanted, and she wasn't sure that she'd give up her creature comforts for the band. She knew that when she sang, when she was on stage, she felt electrified. When she heard the whistles and the applause, she felt loved. But she didn't have Noel's singular passion. She admired him for that. She was even slightly attracted to him for that.

Later, when he'd come into the dressing room, all sweaty and intense, she'd felt that initial spark flare into something else. She wanted what he had. She wanted him.

It had been easy. When Harumi and Esther excused themselves to leave the band in peace for a while, Cassie stayed. She sat on the sofa as John stuck his head under a faucet and then shook his head, spraying water all over. Gretchen did some yoga stretches to unwind, then changed her clothes and went back into the bar. All this time, Noel stood leaning against the wall, watching her.

As soon as they were alone, he crossed the room. He sat down beside her and unzipped her dress. And then they were pawing at each other, sucking, devouring. The whole thing was over in five minutes.

Later, sitting alone and abandoned in the dressing room, after the van had already left, Cassie was sorry. She really hadn't meant to hurt Trudy. But to tell the truth, she had probably done her a favor. Maybe now she'd be able to get him out of her blood and find someone who really loved her. Anyway, she'd apologize. They'd patch things up.

"You got a place for me to stay?" Cassie asked Leo when she found him in the bar. She had changed into a sweatshirt and jeans. The lamé dress was stuffed into her bag again.

"You're still here?" Leo asked.

Cassie nodded. "Trudy and I had a fight. My band left me behind."

He took it all in stride. He was probably used to the crazed antics of musicians. "You can take the Greyhound tomorrow," he said. "I'll even drive you to the station."

Cassie wasn't ready to sleep yet, so when Leo suggested dropping in at a party, she agreed.

An hour later, she found herself in a house with a bunch of other night owls. They probably worked in clubs and restaurants and slept during the day. Leo fell into conversation with some people he knew and Cassie wandered through the rooms on her own. A half-naked couple was making out in one corner. Cassie almost tripped over them. She saw a closed door and knocked. When no one answered, she let herself in.

Two guys and a stubble-headed girl were sitting in a circle. There was a candle at the center. Cassie recognized their gear—the spoon, the belt, the syringe.

The three of them turned their heads in slow motion when she walked into the room.

"Hey," one of the guys said. He was wearing a stocking cap over long greasy black hair. "You're a Screaming Diva. I saw your show tonight. Far out."

"Want to join us?" the other guy asked.

Cassie hesitated for only a moment. Her head was starting to ache. She wanted to forget about the whole scene with Noel. She was no longer part of the band, but she'd deal with that later. Right now she was craving sweet forgetfulness. She wanted that singing in her veins. She moved to the circle, and they made room for her. She sat down and rolled up her sleeve.

40

It was nine o'clock on Sunday morning, and Harumi was sitting on the edge of Esther's bed, the same bed that they had shared during childhood sleepovers. Esther had just opened her eyes, and she thought she might be asleep still, in the midst of some crazy dream.

"Harumi. What are you doing here? How did you get here?"

"Chip gave me a ride," she said. She hooked a long black strand behind her ear and took a deep breath. "I have something to tell you. It's about Cassie."

She's been kicked out of the band, Esther thought with a sinking feeling. Well, then, I'll quit, too. She hadn't been in the dressing room when Trudy had tried to wrap her hands around Cassie's throat, but she'd heard about what had happened. Trudy had raged all the way home about Cassie's betrayal. Or at least it seemed as if Trudy had never shut up. Amazingly, Noel had fallen asleep, but Trudy's anger had unsettled Esther. It had been impossible for her to relax.

Esther couldn't believe that they'd just left her behind. If Cassie had tried to get into the van, she doubted that Trudy would have been able to stop her. After all, it wasn't Trudy's van. Ligeia had rented it for the road trip. But when they were all packed up and ready to roll, Cassie was nowhere in sight.

Esther had worried about her all night. How would she get back to Columbia? Did she have enough money? Would Leo take care of her? Now, struggling into a sitting position in her canopy bed, she heard Harumi say, "It's bad. Are you ready?"

Esther nodded.

Harumi studied her face for a moment. She hadn't looked at Esther so closely in a long time. Even though they'd been together in Trudy's living room for hours on end, Esther felt that they hadn't been in such close proximity in years. "Tell me," she said.

"Cassie went to some party up in DC," Harumi began. She reached out and took Esther's hand in hers. "Leo was with her, I guess, but he ran into some old girlfriend and they went out for coffee and then he lost track of Cassie. There were drugs at this party. Some people were shooting up and Cassie walked in on them and they invited her to join them. And she did."

Esther could feel her bowels freezing. Fear was tightening her chest.

"I don't know exactly what happened," Harumi said. She sniffled then, and reached up to brush away a tear. "She took too many drugs and someone found her in the bathtub. Her skin was all blue. An ambulance came, but she was already dead."

It was impossible, Esther thought. Things like that didn't happen here, not to people that she knew. Dirty strangers OD'ed in dark alleys or abandoned houses. She'd seen it on TV, in movies. Girls like Cassie became airline attendants or movie stars.

"It must have been a mistake," Esther said. She was wide awake now, sitting straight up in the bed. "It must have been someone else, some other blonde girl."

"She's got that scar," Harumi said, touching her own face. "Who else has a scar like that?"

Leo had called Trudy, and then Trudy had called Harumi. Esther wasn't sure if anyone had notified Cassie's parents, but she figured someone had.

"She's—her body's being flown back today," Harumi said. "I guess the funeral will be tomorrow. Maybe Tuesday."

There were tears running down Esther's face now, though no sound came from her throat. She leaned toward Harumi, and Harumi opened her arms. They embraced on the bed.

"I know that she was special to you," Harumi said.

"I loved her. She's the reason I joined the band."

Harumi nodded. "Yeah, me too."

There was no band now. It was all over. They'd never cut a record or be on MTV. No one would ever ask for her autograph. She didn't think she'd ever touch those drums again.

Esther thought that she had never felt so alone in her life. She suddenly wanted to call Rebecca. But then she remembered Harumi. She breathed in Harumi's skin and shampoo. "Thanks for coming over to tell me."

"It was the least I could do," Harumi said. "As your oldest friend."

Later, when she was once again alone in her room, when she'd cried all the tears she could cry, Esther opened her notebook and started to scratch out a song:

SCAR GIRL
She was there on the stage
Spinning in the light
We thought we knew her so well
We thought that we were tight.
But under that skin
Beyond those flashing blue eyes
Her heart was etched with scars
Her cries were stifled by lies.

Where was her mother?
Where was her father?
Where was her lover?
Why didn't we bother?
Scar Girl, we're sorry . . .

41

Harumi stood in front of the mirror in her black dress, staring at her freshly scrubbed face. Should she wear lipstick, or not? Was it better to appear haggard and bereaved, or to make oneself presentable? Harumi didn't know. She'd never been to a funeral before.

Cassie would try to look nice, she thought. She'd cover up her scar and line her blue eyes. Harumi twisted the lipstick tube and smeared on a layer of Passion Punch.

She wondered if she would cry, if her mascara would run. How the hell did she feel, anyway? She couldn't decide. She was in shock, maybe. Grief and sorrow had yet to sink in. Right now she felt something that was oddly like relief. The band would fall apart; she could go back to the violin.

When she was finished with her face, she checked in on Mrs. Harris, found her engrossed in some black-and-white movie on TV, and went outside to wait at the curb for Chip. He had volunteered to accompany her.

It was warm outside, the air full of birdsong and lilacs. The sky was blue. Harumi tried to feel sad, but she couldn't.

Chip's Saab appeared a few minutes later. He jumped out and opened the passenger door for her, escorted her into the car. He was wearing a dark gray suit and a drab, striped tie. He handled her elbow like an egg. "How are you?" His eyebrows scrunched together. "Holding up okay?"

Harumi shook her head. "I don't know. It doesn't seem real."

They didn't speak all the way to the church. Chip left the radio off. Harumi kept flashing through scenes in her mind: Cassie at the lakeside party where they'd first talked, Cassie pounding the stage with her combat boots, Cassie and Trudy laughing in each others' arms. People were saying that Trudy had killed her, had driven her to her death, but Harumi didn't believe it. It had to have been accidental. Trudy would have let her back in the band eventually, no matter what had happened between her and Noel.

The church parking lot was full. There were BMWs and Mercedes Benzes—Cassie's father's friends, Harumi figured. She thought she saw Esther's hatchback off in a corner. Chip parked across the street, in the shade of an oak, and they made their way to the sanctuary.

The pews were full of kids from school. They probably hadn't even known Cassie, but here they were, wallowing in the melodrama. Sobs broke through the mellow organ music. One girl was near hysteria. Trudy was up in the front. She was wearing dark glasses, as if she didn't want to be recognized. Adam was nowhere in sight. Neither was Noel.

The mahogany coffin was open at the altar. Cassie's blonde hair shone in the light. Her cheeks were a little too rosy. Sleeping Beauty, Harumi thought. Any minute now, she'll sit up and start singing "Lady Lazarus Rises Again."

Chip stood beside her, as solid as granite. She led him to the front and slid in next to Trudy.

"Hey," she whispered.

Trudy nodded slightly. Her jaw was clenched. Harumi realized that she'd been crying. The dark glasses were for hiding tears. Harumi laced her fingers through Trudy's and they sat there in silence.

She could make out the faint smile on the waxen corpse. Did Cassie die like that, or had the undertaker crafted her expression? Harumi shuddered. She wished someone would bring down the lid.

Harumi saw Cassie's father in the front pew with his young wife. A few months before, Cassie had predicted their divorce, but here they were together, leaning on each other like fellow cripples. Funny how these things brought people together. Harumi couldn't help thinking of her own parents. What if it had been her instead? Would they be as wrecked as Cassie's father appeared to be? Or would they suffer stoically, according to some Japanese code of decorum? Maybe they were here somewhere, in a gesture of community solidarity. She would call them after this. She'd tell them what had happened and she'd invite them to meet Chip. She was almost ready to forgive them.

Esther slipped into the pew. Chip moved over so the Divas could sit together. Harumi held out her free hand, but instead of taking it, Esther handed her a folded piece of paper. She raised her eyebrows.

"Read it," Esther mouthed, sitting.

Harumi pulled her other hand away from Trudy and opened the paper. She could tell right away that it was a song, a ballad. The first stanza brought fresh tears to her eyes. She tapped out the beat of the words on her knee. A melody began to form in her head. Everyone rose to their feet for a hymn, but Harumi could barely hear the organ. All she heard was the song in her head. The Divas would have to stick together at least long enough to perform this song. They had to do this one thing for Cassie.

The ceremony passed in a blur. Afterward, they followed the other mourners to the Haywood house. The living room was crammed. Harumi picked out Ms. Claiborne, the high school English teacher. There were a bunch of kids from school with their parents, including, oddly enough, Todd Elsworth, that jock she'd escaped from at the party.

"Maybe we should offer our condolences," Esther said.

Johnette was carrying a tray of drinks. Harumi hadn't noticed before, but her dress was just tight enough to show off a swelling at her middle. She was obviously pregnant. They would go on, Dex and Johnette, with their new family. They would take down Cassie's photos and put them in a box. She would become a ghost, like her mother.

"Maybe . . . ." Esther prodded again.

"Yeah, let's go," Trudy said. The three of them linked arms and went over to Cassie's father, who was leaning against the doorjamb. His suit was immaculately pressed, but his face was furrowed. He looked as if he hadn't slept in days. Harumi detected a whiff of Scotch. How Cassie would have hated that smell. He stared blankly at the three of them, there in front of him.

Harumi spoke up first. "Um, Mr. Haywood, we're sorry for your loss."

He nodded and gulped. "Are you friends of hers? School friends?"

They all nodded.

"She was our guitar player," Trudy blurted out.

"We were in a band together," Harumi said quietly. "We called ourselves Screaming Divas."

His face started to crumple. "Why didn't I know that?"

Trudy shrugged. "I guess you weren't paying attention."

"I guess you're right." He took a deep breath and composed himself. "Look, why don't you go into her room and take something to remember her by. Take whatever you want."

They looked at each other and nodded. "Thank you, sir."

The last time they'd been in that room, the bed had been unmade and clothes had been strewn all over the place. Cassie's textbooks had been in a leaning tower on the floor. Today, everything was neat and orderly.

Harumi and Trudy watched as Esther slowly pulled back the quilt and lifted the pillow to her face. She inhaled deeply, then threw it back down. "It smells like Downy," she murmured. "There's no trace of her at all."

No doubt within a few days, Johnette would have all this stuff bagged and sent off to Goodwill. Then they could get busy putting up a wallpaper border with ducklings or whatever.

Esther crouched down in front of Cassie's bookcase. After a moment, she pulled out *The Collected Poems* by Sylvia Plath and held it against her heart.

Harumi's eyes roved slowly around the room, taking in the portrait of her mom in beauty queen regalia, the Doc Martens and ballet flats lined up under the bed, the bottles of fingernail polish on the vanity. Then something caught her eye—Cassie's sparkly pink guitar pick, nestled in a crystal tray. Harumi reached down and plucked it out. She held it for a moment, remembering how it had caught the light when she played, before tucking it in her skirt pocket.

Now it was Trudy's turn. Without a moment's hesitation, she claimed the guitar propped in the corner. "Okay," she said, clutching it by the neck. "Let's get out of here. This place is starting to give me the creeps."

42

When Trudy stumbled into her rented house the night of the funeral, she was totally wasted. She'd broken into her father's apartment and helped herself to a fifth of whiskey. Her dad was apparently off somewhere on vacation.

She didn't know why she'd gone to him. He wasn't the "kiss it and make it better" type. Yet she'd wanted something a little familiar and comforting to counteract the shock of Cassie's death. When he wasn't there, she'd felt like vandalizing his place. Instead, she'd just filched the liquor.

Her answering machine at home was full of malicious messages, left by fans of Screaming Divas—fans of Cassie. Some of them were threats, others just prolonged sobbing. And then there was that other message.

"You bitch!" one of the callers, some high school girl, no doubt, had wailed. "You killed her. I hope you go to hell."

Yeah, she was probably headed there anyhow, but who cared? It was no doubt more interesting than sitting around on a bunch of puffy clouds listening to harps. That's what she told people, anyhow. She didn't really believe in all that.

No one seemed to understand that she'd loved Cassie. They'd been like sisters, like halves of one self. She'd felt their personalities oozing together at times. Maybe that's why she'd screwed Noel. They'd both been involved with Adam, they shared songs, why not share Noel, too? It made sense in a weird sort of way, but when she'd seen them together, she'd totally lost it. Maybe she was afraid that they would team up and leave her behind, when she needed them both.

She hadn't talked to Noel since they'd returned from Washington, DC. Right now she didn't think she could stand the sight of his face. She wanted to see Cassie and plan the future of their band.

Among the rants and slurs on her answering machine, there was another message that she'd played over and over:

"Hey, Trudy? This is your mama calling from Los Angeles. You're probably not going to believe this, but I've been temping for Wild Blue Records and I handed your demo to the A & R guy. That's Artists and Repertoire, by the way. And guess what? He was impressed. He said y'all had a lot of energy and he wants to hear more." There was a long pause before she went on. "And Trudy, I'd really like to see you. Why don't you come on out here and give us a visit?"

Sarah must not have heard about Cassie, and that was just as well. She'd have to find a replacement for Cassie, and maybe for Esther and Harumi, too, if they were giving up on her. But Trudy had put so much into this band that she wasn't about to quit now. She would carry on as a tribute to the lost Diva.

It was midnight in South Carolina, but still suppertime on the west coast. Trudy listened to the message once again, scratching down her mother's new phone number. Then she erased the other messages. She stabbed out the digits with her index finger and waited for the ring.

"Hey, Ma," she said, practicing. "My suitcase is already packed. When can you pick me up?"

ABOUT THE AUTHOR

Back in the day, Suzanne Kamata spent a lot of time hanging out in a club in Columbia, South Carolina, much like the one in this book. (The Beat goes on . . . .) She later wrote about musicians for the *State* newspaper, the *Japan Times*, and other publications. Now, she mostly writes novels. In her free time, she enjoys searching for the perfect fake fur leopard print coat and listening to the Japanese all-girl band Chatmonchy.